THE ADVENTURES OF

DODGE DALTON

AGAINST THE

FALL OF ETERNAL NIGHT

SEAN ELLIS
WITH KERRY FREY

PRAISE FOR SEAN ELLIS

"*The Outpost of Fate proves that Dodge Dalton is a worthy heir to Indiana Jones, Dirk Pitt and the classic action adventure heroes of yore. A page-turner, from beginning to end!*" – Barry Reese, author of THE ROOK CHRONICLES.

"*An adrenaline-fueled joyride through adventure! Ellis hits his stride at The Outpost of Fate, juggling familiar heroes and new villains with ease, and his plotting is a thrill-a-second, escalating toward an intriguing collision of ancient myth and modern science. This one will leave you hungry for more – and in no hurry to 'get out of Dodge'.*" – David Sakmyster, author of THE PHAROS OBJECTIVE and CRESCENT LAKE.

"*Exotic settings, despicable villains, stalwart heroes, and a pace that never lets up . . . Sean Ellis's THE ADVENTURES OF DODGE DALTON AT THE OUTPOST OF FATE gives you everything you'd ever want in a top-notch adventure yarn! If you're a fan of James Rollins and Clive Cussler, you really need to be reading Sean Ellis.*" – James Reasoner, author of REDEMPTION, KANSAS.

"*Sean Ellis is a thriller reader's dream come true.*" – Jeremy Robinson, author of PULSE, INSTINCT, and THRESHOLD.

"*Anyone who grew up reading adventure stories from the pulps will relish Ellis' affectionate evocation of the era and his unapologetically old-fashioned storytelling. It's yarns like his that got me into the adventuring game, and I'm delighted to see them still being penned.*" – Gabriel Hunt, author of HUNT AT THE WELL OF ETERNITY and HUNT THROUGH THE CRADLE OF FEAR.

OTHER THRILLERS BY SEAN ELLIS

Mira Raiden Adventures
Ascendant
Descendant

The Nick Kismet Thrillers
The Shroud of Heaven
Into the Black
Fortune Favors
The Devil You Know (novella)

The Adventures of Dodge Dalton
In the Shadow of Falcon's Wings
At the Outpost of Fate
On the High Road to Oblivion
Against the Fall of Eternal Night

The John Thomas Rourke Survival Academy
Camp Zero

Chess Team/Jack Sigler Thrillers
(with Jeremy Robinson)
Callsign: King
Underworld
Blackout
Prime
Savage
Herculean

The Jade Ihara Adventures
(with David Wood)
Oracle
Changeling

Other Works
Magic Mirror
WarGod (with Steven Savile)
Hell Ship (with David Wood)
Destiny (with David Wood)
Flood Rising (with Jeremy Robinson)

...IN THE GOLDEN AGE OF ADVENTURE...

PROLOGUE — WHERE ANGELS TREAD

The man ran as fast as his aging legs would allow. He took a deep breath, squeezing the neck of the heavy burlap sack that hung over his right shoulder as if it was a lifeline. In a way, that wasn't far from the truth, though it was not the bag itself but rather what was in it that he clung to.

It was also an anchor, weighing him down when he needed so desperately to flee.

A sound, a low atonal hum like the protracted echo of his exhalations, penetrated the desert air, building toward a crescendo. Getting closer. Fear surged through him, giving him the strength to keep going.

Where was that sound coming from?

Blood trickled down from his earlobes, drip, drip, dripping onto his shoulders. He reached up and pulled a traditional *keffiyeh* from his head. He was not a Bedouin, but he had long ago learned the wisdom of dressing in the fashion of the desert dwellers. The cloth head scarf was soaked with sweat and dotted with some of his blood. He pressed it to his bleeding ears, first the right and then the left, and was alarmed at the size of the stain that came away. He did not even know he had been injured. When had it happened? He wrapped the cloth around his head once again, more a bandage now than a covering to protect him from the scorching sun.

He climbed a dune, half-crawling, half-swimming against the sliding sands. Pain, like nothing he had ever felt before, burned through his muscles, but he kept going, crested the top, and then tumbled down the other side.

He lay at the bottom of the slope for a long moment, trying to motivate himself into motion again, but the bright burning disk of the sun had become murderous, robbing him of both strength and the will to remain conscious.

There it was again, that awful sound.

Now he remembered. Not the same sound at all, but similar enough that he could not help but be drawn back to that moment when he had fled the ruin and broken faith. The memory of the sound, a deep, resonant thrum, like distant thunder, shuddered anew through every fiber of his being, filling his mind with images of skulls and hungry demons, but these were not hallucinations brought on by exposure and dehydration. These were memories of the place from which he was fleeing.

The horrible visages leered at him from the midst of the roiling convection waves. That sound! That terrible sound that had vibrated through him like a wire about to snap. It was different this time, not in the pitch or rhythm, but rather in its intensity. In the chamber below the ruins, it had been focused, amplified. Out here in the open, it was… tolerable.

There had been another sound too, a shriek of terror. Not his, but the person he had left behind.

His name, Sadiki, meant "faithful" and "loyal." *I have dishonored my own name*, he thought. *I left her there to die!*

An ominous cloud fell over him like a harbinger of doom. He opened his eyes, but the silhouette blocking the sun was just a dark spot overhead. The moment of shade was all the respite he would be given. He tried to steady his breathing. Sweat and blood stung his eyes and blurred his vision, but he could see the black outlines of birds in the sky. Vultures, gathering to feast on his flesh.

He loosened the string around the sack and rooted inside until he felt the artifact, mixed in with other baubles. He ran his fingers over the smooth amulet and recalled again the faces of the demon gods who had guarded the chamber. Perhaps the vultures were the servants of Anubis or Osiris, come to exact punishment for his transgression.

Not today, he told himself. *I will not die today.*

He closed the sack and struggled to his feet. A gentle breeze broke from the west, making the sand shimmer and dance around him, but the shadow of the birds remained with him as he pushed onward, swooshing around him in a hypnotic pattern. He fought to keep his eyes off the sky and the dread that hovered above and fixed his gaze on the horizon where he thought he could see palm trees.

Palm trees meant water, and water meant life.

Over the persistent rushing noise, he caught the sound of camels braying up ahead. He dropped flat on the blistering sand, shrinking into the desert to avoid being seen by the Bedouins who surely accompanied them. Perhaps they were friendly, perhaps not. It was a chance he dared not take, not with what he carried.

The sound came again, echoing across the desert sand, and this time, he was not the only one to have heard it.

The camels began to struggle against their tethers, braying louder, alarmed by the sudden noise. The men—six of them in all—drew swords and rifles and moved out to form a perimeter around their herd. Their weapons, like their stares, were directed skyward.

Sadiki wiped the sweat and blood from his face and crawled for the shelter of the dune. He had just reached it when one of the birds swooped silently out of the sky and dived at the caravan. The report of a rifle echoed across the desert followed immediately by a terrified scream.

Sadiki looked back and saw a Bedouin man fall to the sand, or rather the top half of the man. He had been sliced in half at the waist.

Sadiki covered his mouth to silence his own scream. *Allah be merciful,* he thought.

The Bedouin's severed lower body staggered a few steps forward and then toppled over onto the sand. A second bird swooped down from the formation, another close behind it. There was a flash of movement and an eruption of blood as a second man went down. One by one, all six were cut down in matter of seconds.

The birds circled their kills and then glided down to land on the sand near their victims. They settled to the ground in a nearly perfect line, like a military formation, their backs to Sadiki.

He realized two things in that moment. First, he was certain that they had not seen him because he was still alive. Second, they were neither birds nor demons sent by Osiris, but men, dressed in clinging black outfits. On their backs were great wings made of what appeared to be razor-sharp metal feathers, stained with the blood of the Bedouins they had slain. The wings were now folded behind them, making them look like grim avenging angels.

The cloud passed over the sun again, the hum growing louder. He peered up and this time saw it clearly. A giant dirigible floated in the sky. It was silver-gray in color, more than two hundred feet long with an under-slung gondola and four large outboard engines. The noise, so like and yet also unlike the sound that still haunted him, was the sound of those engines churning at full speed. The aircraft hung above him and then began to nose down, toward the waiting bird-men.

As it descended, Sadiki could see no marking of nationality, but he could see men moving about in the gondola slung beneath the gas envelope. Long mooring ropes trailed from the cabin and the nose and tail of the dirigible. The birdmen on the ground raced forward to grasp the ropes with their hands, and as they pulled it down, the engines fell quiet.

Sadiki watched in amazement as the giant ship was pulled down so that the gondola touched the desert floor. When the hawkmen had the craft secure, a door opened in the gondola, and a figure emerged, a tall man, his features hidden beneath the hood of the long dark cloak he wore. He was dragging something…no, someone, an old man whom he pulled out of the gondola and dropped on the sand.

"Useless," raged a voice from beneath the hood. He stood over the old man and placed a foot on his chest. "I should crush you like the cockroach you are."

Sadiki could see the old man wincing, struggling to breathe. He was injured, but even if he had been in full health, Sadiki knew he would have been incapable of fighting back. The supine man in the brown tweed coat, with the wild silver hair and the high-pitched voice, was a man of books and learning, not a man of violence.

"If I did not require your services, I would leave you thus." The hooded man pointed to the hacked apart bodies scattered nearby, then he reached down and raised Professor Padraig Dunn off the ground, lifting him until the professor's feet dangled several inches above the sand.

Is this possible? Sadiki thought. *Can one man truly have that much strength?*

"Find the Door of Osiris, professor," the hooded man shouted. "Find it before the moon turns full."

The hooded man released Dunn, letting him collapse limp on the sand. He whirled toward the dirigible, but then turned back toward to the tormented man. "If you do not, your family will suffer the fate I have shown you. You will watch your daughter cut in two, and then you will join her in Hell!"

The hooded man entered the gondola, followed by several of the hawkmen who, one by one, filed toward the airship with their ropes in hand, releasing them just before climbing aboard. The dirigible rose into the afternoon sky, taking with it the last four men who still clung to their ropes. The engines roared to life, the propellers spinning faster as the ship gained altitude. When it was several hundred feet above the earth, the remaining hawkmen let go of their ropes and began swooping and gliding through the sky again, only this time, they did not descend. Instead, they flew back under the envelope and came to rest alongside it, like pigeons roosting. Then, they too disappeared inside as the mighty ship continued to ascend, making its way toward the distant horizon.

Sadiki waited several minutes before moving toward the scene of the massacre where he found the Dunn sitting up.

Sadiki embraced the man. He felt impotent in the face of such evil. "Professor, what have they done?"

"Sadiki?" the professor asked, catching his breath and grasping the man. "Is it truly you, my faithful servant?"

"You are hurt." He could now see the professor's wounds: contusions across his face, eyes swollen and bloody.

"They beat me," he said, turning upwards toward his friend. "Rather badly, I'm afraid. But never mind that. What happened to you? Where is my daughter?"

Guilt wrenched at Sadiki's heart. "I—I do not know, Professor. I fear she has been lost. You see, we found it."

Dunn's hand tightened on Sadiki's arm. "The Door of Osiris?"

"It was in the Hidden Valley, exactly where you said it would be," Sadiki replied, unable to completely hide his satisfaction at the accomplishment, despite the terrible cost of the discovery. As if it would explain better than any words he might possess, Sadiki reached into the burlap sack and brought out the artifact. He held it close so the professor could make out the markings that adorned its smooth surface.

"My amulet?" breathed Dunn.

"When she...your daughter... I warned her not to, but she..." Sadiki slumped in defeat.

"She went through? Then you do not know for certain that she is dead?"

The cautious optimism in Dunn's voice was almost unbearable.

"She must be," Sadiki said, miserably.

Dunn's swollen eyes narrowed in what might have been grief. He reached a hand to Sadiki's head. "You're bleeding,"

"I will live, professor." He paused, proffering the amulet. "Is this what that man, the enemy, seeks?"

The professor looked the artifact over closely, tracing his fingers over the fine engraving. Sadiki was unfamiliar with the metal, but he certainly recognized the design—a column, tapering toward the top, with four horizontal crosspieces.

"It is the sign of Osiris," Dunn said. "A talisman to resurrect the dead. The key to the Underworld, opening the night passage so that Ra may travel to the land of the sunrise." He sighed. "But to answer your question, yes. He seeks to open the Door and journey into the realm of Osiris."

Sadiki thought about the terrible things he had glimpsed at the edge of the chamber…the threshold of the Door of Osiris. "What man would willingly choose to go into that place?"

"A man who is not a man," Dunn said in a haunted voice. Then a sad smile crossed his face. "And my daughter, apparently. So like her to rush in where angels fear to tread."

"What should we do?"

"That fool threatens to take from me the one thing I have already lost. If he could bring Fiona back, I would gladly give him what he wants."

"And if he gets what he wants? What happens then?"

"Terrible things." Dunn straightened. "We must get to New York. Those camels. Do you think they can carry us to civilization?"

"New York? In America? Why would we go there?"

"There is a man there, a scientist. A friend of my daughter. He is a leading expert on rare metals such as this." He shook the amulet. "He may be able to help us figure out how to defeat that madman. And he may be able to help us…" Dunn's voice trailed off.

"Yes?" Sadiki shook his head in confusion. "Help us with what?"

Dunn gripped Sadiki's arm. "Help us bring Fiona back."

SS Obergruppenführer Wilhelm Kaufmann sat at the head of a huge, magnificent table made from petrified wood. A large man, with the chiseled frame of an athlete, he had black hair, oily skin and a face scarred from untreated adolescent acne. He was alone in the conference room, a rare moment of solitude for someone at his level of responsibility.

It did not last long, but then he knew it would not.

The door opened and a group of men strode in. They wore street clothes, more precisely, clothes that would not look out of place on the streets of Berlin or Munich—cotton shirts with precisely knotted ties, lightweight business suits, broad-brimmed fedoras—but which definitely set them apart from the Arab rabble that swarmed the back alleys of Cairo. Yet, the clothes could not hide the men that they were. Their proud, exquisitely disciplined bearing marked them all as soldiers of the highest caliber, even when they did not wear the uniform of the Schutzstaffel.

Except for the man at center of the group, a wiry man, an Arab, but one that had allowed himself to be domesticated by his British colonial masters. He was dressed in a silk suit, with large black-framed spectacles and a Borsalino fedora. The contempt that twisted his bearded face adequately expressed his displeasure at being summoned to stand before Kaufmann, but as soon as he reached the table, he made his feelings explicit.

"Kaufmann! How dare you?"

Kaufman leaned back in his chair. "We had an arrangement, Hassan. Imagine how disappointed I was to learn that you were interfering with the research my scientific team is conducting."

"The Museum agreed to let you do research with the artifacts, not remove them. No matter what terms you think we've agreed to, the antiquities belong to Egypt, and here they will remain. It will take more than you and your gang of hooligans to get us to change our minds."

"Hooligans?" Kaufmann raised an eyebrow, allowing his gaze to drift to the hard faces of his men. "These are the finest, professional soldiers that Deutschland has to offer. You insult them with such impertinent language."

Hassan leaned in to the table, his face already red with barely restrained rage. "You and your so-called professional soldiers are nothing more than criminals, Kaufmann. You think Egypt will just bow to your demands? Well, I'm here to tell you that that will not happen. Not today, not any day."

Kaufmann took a black leather riding crop from the tabletop and held the ends in either hand, flexing it in the middle. "I feel that you have perhaps misunderstood the very generous terms of our agreement." He flicked his wrist, and the crop swished the air with a tearing sound. "Perhaps, a reminder is in order."

"The museum will not be coerced with threats, Kaufmann.

Kaufmann snapped the crop again, this time so sharply that it cracked in the air. Hassan flinched.

"Perhaps not," Kaufmann replied. "But will you?"

Hassan stiffened and made a dismissive and, if Kaufmann's knowledge of the culture was accurate, quite rude gesture with his left hand and then wheeled around as if to leave.

"*Erhalten ihn!*" Kaufmann shouted.

Two of his men bolted forward and grabbed Hassan before he could take a step. They held him with a strong firm grip, while a third delivered a punch to the Arab's stomach that doubled him over.

Suddenly, the door flew open, and two more of Kaufmann's men entered the room dragging an Arab woman by her hair. She wore a simple dress, white with a pattern of colorful flowers. One hand clung to a matching hijab. The head scarf had been torn away, along with her dignity. She was middle-aged, but would still probably be considered beautiful by local standards. Of course, Kaufmann was no judge. All that mattered was that Hassan still desired her.

Her captors threw her to the floor in front of the Arab man.

Hassan gave a wail of desperation, but was immediately silenced by another punch to the gut. He gasped for air, curling over like a worm on a fishhook.

"Perhaps now the terms of our agreement shall come into better focus," Kaufmann said as he rose and walked over to the woman. He cracked the crop a few inches in front of her face.

Tears streamed down the woman's face. Kaufmann bent down and cupped the woman's chin in his left hand. He caressed the woman's face with the crop, touching the end to her lips. "She has very beautiful skin."

Kaufmann felt the hatred radiating from Hassan. *What's the old saying,* he thought. *If looks could kill...?* He looked up at the man, smiled, and then slashed the crop across Hassan's face. The sound cracked like a pistol. Even the guards winced. Hassan's glasses flew in pieces across the room, shattering against the wall. A red weal, oozing blood, marked the man's cheek and the bridge of his nose. Hassan tried to reach up to the wound, but Kaufmann's men continued to hold him fast.

"I am not a cruel man, Hassan. You see? I have not damaged your wife's beautiful skin. It would pain me to do so. Do I make my meaning clear, or do I need to be more explicit?"

Hassan shook his head. Fat drops of blood flew from the tip of his nose and splattered the floor.

"Excellent!" Kaufmann turned to his men. "Remove these vermin from my sight."

The men dragged Hassan and his wife from the room, the former leaving streaks of blood in his wake. Kaufmann shook his head wearily. Being the leader of an elite Sicherheitsdienst research team was a messy job sometimes.

"Obergruppenführer!"

Kaufmann raised his eyes to the man rushing into the room. Younger than the other SS soldiers but no less an exquisite specimen of human perfection, the man hastened to him and stood at attention, awaiting the go ahead.

"Yes? What is it?"

The young man handed him the note and returned to attention, clicking his boot against the wooden floor.

Kaufmann read the note carefully, then read it again to make sure that he understood what his superior officer, Heinrich Himmler, Reichsfuhrer of the SS, was telling him to do. Without looking at the messenger, he said, "Please show Professor Novotny and his staff in."

"Jawohl!"

Kaufmann frowned. Dealing with the insect Hassan would not, it seemed, be the most unpleasant thing he would do today, but orders were orders.

The door opened and a tall, thin man strode in. Novotny was not young, but not as old as his white hair would suggest. He wore a long brown double-breasted duster coat, cinched at the waist with a belt like a trench coat. He also wore gloves, and despite being indoors, dark sunglasses with circular frames. A cloth scarf, smudged with sand and grit, circled his neck below his bearded chin as if it had just been removed from covering his mouth and nose.

"Welcome, Professor Novotny. I am SS Obergruppenführer Wilhelm Kaufmann."

Novotny removed his gloves and placed them in the pockets of his coat, then doffed his sunglasses, revealing startlingly colorless eyes. Kaufmann found he could not bear to meet the man's gaze, so he looked away, gesturing to the table. "Please, sit, Professor Novotny. You appear to have just come in from a long journey. I will have some refreshments brought in."

Novotny sat, but said nothing.

"The Reichsfuhrer sends a rather glowing introduction of your background and expertise. I believe you will be a brilliant addition to our team."

"I am not here to work for you, Kaufmann," Novotny said. Despite his Slavic heritage, he spoke English with no discernible accent. "Quite the opposite. You are now working for me."

Kaufmann managed, barely, to hide his dismay, keeping his expression neutral. "And what it is that the Reichsfuhrer wants me to do for you?"

"Blitzkrieg."

"I'm sorry?"

"Lightning warfare. Your Fuhrer means to unleash a storm upon the world." Novotny stared at Kaufmann, forcing the SS officer to look away again. "In the desert, not far from Farafra Oasis, there is a temple. In this temple is an artifact of unparalleled power that will win this war that your Fuhrer means to unleash."

"Of course," Kaufmann said, quickly. He had heard talk of this sort before. He was not a believer in mysticism, but the men who gave him his orders were. If they demanded amulets and talismans revered by long-extinct cultures, it was not his place to question. "If it is there to be found, we will find it."

"I will find it. That is not your concern."

"I don't understand."

"No, you don't." A cryptic smile bent Novotny's lips. "But you will."

The Adventures of Dodge Dalton

Chapter Twelve—Fight Fire with Fire

Dodge Dalton and Molly Rose Shannon rush through the
doors into the main keep of Boroff's stronghold. It
is an old castle hall, decorated with suits of armor
and old-fashioned weapons—swords, maces, pole-axes—
mounted to the walls. A stairway spirals around the
interior wall, rising to a balcony where Boroff
stands, looking down. A heavy chandelier, holding
dozens of burning candles, hangs above the center of
the room, suspended by a thick rope which rises into
the shadows overhead and then angles down to a cleat
on the wall midway up the stairs. Directly below the
chandelier, tied on the table like a sacrificial
offering, is the unconscious form of Hurricane Hurley. Boroff's chief henchman, the gigantic mute
Thorg, is just cinching the last of the ropes when
Dodge and Molly storm in.

Boroff shouts, "Get them!"

Six of Boroff's lesser minions race down the steps
to intercept Dodge and Molly. Thorg however grabs a
torch and heads up the stairs as if fleeing the battle, but he isn't running away.

"Dodge!" Molly cries. "He's going to drop the chandelier on Hurricane. We've got to save him."

Sure enough, that's what Thorg intends, but
Boroff's men are between them and the giant who
threatens their friend.

Fists fly. Dodge socks one man, then another. Molly
grabs a vase off a side-table and cracks it down on

the head of a third, and then slugs another across the jaw, knocking him out cold as Dodge deals with the last two.

With them out of the way, Dodge races up the steps, just as Thorg is about to set fire to the rope. The giant turns to meet his charge, swiping the air with the torch, forcing Dodge to retreat a few steps. He sees a pair of crossed sabers on the wall and grabs one, thrusting it at Thorg, driving him back, away from the rope. Dodge swings the blade again, but Thorg parries with the torch. The saber cuts through the brand, but the impact knocks the sword out of Dodge's grasp and it clatters down the steps. Now both men are unarmed, but despite the Thorg's enormous size, Dodge doesn't hesitate. He leaps forward, tackling Thorg and wrestling him off the stairs. Together, they crash down onto the Hurricane's unconscious body, hitting with such force that the table legs snap and the top crashes to the floor.

Hurricane's eyes flutter open. He pulls at his bonds and succeeds in loosening one of them with a mighty heave, even as Dodge and Thorg continue to grapple amidst the ruins of the table.

Meanwhile, Boroff sensing that his plan is about to come apart, rushes down the stairs. He grabs the second saber from the wall and heads back up to the rope, intent on slashing it and dropping the chandelier onto Dodge and Hurricane, sacrificing Thorg if necessary, to ensure the end of Dodge Dalton.

Molly sees what's about to happen and dashes to the steps, snatching up the sword Dodge dropped earlier. Boroff is already sawing at the rope. The fibers are parting one by one, faster as the rope weakens and the remaining fibers are strained to the breaking point. Molly lunges at Boroff, driving him back. He parries with the saber. Steel rings against steel.

While Molly and Boroff fight on the steps, Dodge is caught in a crushing bear hug. He struggles but Thorg is too powerful. Then, a table legs breaks over Thorg's head.

Hurricane, still trying to get loose, manages to stun Thorg long enough for Dodge to wriggle free. But it will take more than that to stop the hulking Thorg. Hurricane holds Thorg's arms, preventing him from renewing his attack on Dodge, while Dodge throws punches at the giant's face. It's like hitting a block of marble.

Overhead, the chandelier begins to sway and drops an inch as the rope starts to break, one fiber at a time.

Molly and Boroff continue to fence on the steps. She is a skilled fighter but not as experienced as Boroff. He drives her back with a flurry of blows which she is barely able to parry, but he's not trying to win. He wants to cut the rope. When he gets close enough, he raises his blade and slashes at the damaged spot, cutting the rope in two.

The chandelier falls.

Dodge, seeing what's about to happen, clambers over Thorg and drags Hurricane away from the wreckage of the table a moment before the chandelier smashes down, crushing Thorg to oblivion. Flames flare up as the topped candles set fire to the table.

Molly cries out and lunges forward, running Boroff through with her saber. He stiffens, breathes a dying curse, and then topples off the stairs, into the flames that are now spreading across the floor.

Then Dodge rushes out of the fire and charges up the steps.

"Oh, Dodge!" Molly cries out. "You're alive!"

"We won't be for long." He races up, the flames devouring the stairs right behind him, and hugs her.

Without a moment to lose, he grabs the severed end of the chandelier rope and, with Molly still in his embrace, swings out over the flames to land on the far side where Hurricane is waiting to catch them.

"Hurricane! You're alive!" Molly says, throwing her arms around him.

"I'm like a bad penny, Miss Molly. I always turn up. Now, let's get out of here before we get roasted."

Outside, the three race across the drawbridge while the castle burns behind them. Once they are on the far side, Dodge and Molly embrace.

They kiss.

Molly gazes up into his eyes. "I love you, Dodge Dalton."

He looks into her eyes and says….

"You have got to be kidding me!"

CHAPTER 1 — HOORAY FOR HOLLYWOOD

The troop of soldiers, all wearing uniforms that looked suspiciously like the attire of the German army, froze in mid step as they backed out of the ancient temple, brandishing their machine guns at the monstrosities emerging from the shadowy depths from which they had just retreated.

It was an army of the undead.

Monsters wrapped in ancient burial cloths edged their way through the opening. Mummies, dozens of them hinting at the possibility of hundreds more to follow, their wrappings, torn and filthy from thousands of years of decay, shuffled toward the soldiers, clawing past one another in their haste to feast on the living.

An officer wearing a Tropenhelm cap, his hand raised, poised to give the command to fire, abruptly turned his head in the direction of the shout, and then swore angrily at the disturbance.

"Cu-u-u-u-t!" shouted the director, stretching the word out, pitch rising with each protracted syllable.

David Dalton—"Dodge" to his friends—winced and looked up guiltily from the typed pages that had prompted his outburst, but it was too late. The damage was already done.

The director, a compact pugnacious man by the name of Jack English sprang from his folding chair and pointed a finger at Dodge. "Get off my set!"

A hulking uniformed figure stationed near the door lurched into motion, like one of the mummies summoned to life by an ancient curse, but the woman sitting next to Dodge immediately raised her hand.

"No need to get your hands dirty, Mop," Elizabeth Sansom said quickly, her brisk California accent making the words sound like a barrage of incoming machine gun fire "I'll take care of him."

She turned to Dodge, her look of disgust almost as severe as the one worn by English. "Come on, sport. Let's get you out of here before you ruin any more perfectly good film stock. It's not cheap you know."

Dodge worked his mouth to protest, but a glance at the still-advancing hulking security guard with the unlikely nickname "Mop," convinced him that retreat was the only viable option. He hastened after the woman who had interceded in his behalf.

As they moved off, Dodge heard English calling out again, addressing the cast in that strange idiom which, over the course of the last few days, Dodge had found himself immersed in: the language of moving picture production.

Hollywood was like a foreign country to him, stranger than all the other places he had been put together. Of course, that wasn't surprising given that the Republic Studios backlot contained sets for the production of jungle adventures, Wild West shoot 'em ups, and medieval epics. Even stranger were the people. Everyone was beautiful and in a hurry, and about as phony as the mummies that were getting ready to menace the equally ersatz soldiers of the Black Legion on the set behind him.

What am I doing here? He wondered not for the first time.

By all rights, he should have been thrilled at the possibility that someone—and not just any someone, but media mogul Herbert J. Yates— wanted to turn his stories into motion pictures. Back when he thought they were just stories, he would have been. Now he knew better.

Three years ago, Dodge, a sports writer for the Clarion in New York City, had been given the unlikely assignment of transforming the very purple prose of one Brian "Hurricane" Hurley into something a little more publishable. Dodge had done exactly that, transforming Hurricane's stories, which were purportedly the true adventures of international crime-fighter Captain Zane Falcon and his men—a roster that included the original author—into the very successful syndicated weekly feature *The Adventures of Captain Falcon*. Then something had happened that eclipsed any joy he might have derived from that triumph. Dodge had learned the truth about Captain Falcon and his adventures. Hurricane Hurley's stories weren't just stories.

In the months that followed that revelation, Dodge had been thrust into the role of world-saving adventure hero, dealing with enemies and threats that surpassed even his own imagination.

The victories had been costly. Dodge had suffered more heartbreak than he cared to think about, and gone from famous to infamous and back again so many times that he no longer bothered trying to keep track of his public image.

The latest, and most unexpected development had come just a few weeks earlier, when his editor, Max Beardsley, had announced his intention to discontinue *The Adventures of Captain Falcon*, and begin publishing in its place, *The Real Adventures of Dodge Dalton*, with Dodge's involvement in the new series limited to the use of his name and the odd public appearance. Following close on the heels of that bombshell was an invitation to visit Republic Pictures studio in California, to consult on the production of a motion picture serial based on the new series.

"Consult" was film industry talk for giving a stamp of approval to the production. He would not be offering any real input, just showing up and making an appearance.

Dodge's initial reaction had been to crumple the invitation up and pitch it in the wastebasket. Not only did a trip to Hollywood to advise a film crew making a movie ostensibly based on his own life seem extraordinarily frivolous and self-serving, but he had much bigger problems to worry about.

After further contemplation however, he realized that maybe a day or two away from those problems was exactly what he needed, so he dug the letter out of the trash and made a phone call.

He'd been greeted in California by the hot Santa Ana winds and a hired car that delivered him to Studio City where he had met the hulking Mop, wearing a uniform that looked like it might have been used in one of Mack Sennett's slapstick police films. Dodge would later learn that the Keystone Kops motion pictures had been filmed at this very location.

His initial meeting with Elizabeth—"call me Liz"—Sansom had gone well enough. She was pretty, with light brown hair just a shade darker than his own, a pert nose and sparkling brown eyes, but it had not been long before the friction started. Most of it was creative, but not all.

Jack English's black Packard One-Twenty automobile was parked at the edge of the cave set where the exterior shots of the Black Legion episode were being filmed. Liz waited until they were just past the vehicle before unleashing her pent up anger. "Would you care to explain what you meant back there?"

He shook his head. "Sorry. I forgot where I was. I'm not used to the rules of movie making"

"I'm not talking about that." She put her hands on her hips, defiant. "What exactly is wrong with my story?"

Dodge was taken aback by the ire in her tone. He had almost forgotten about the script treatment that had prompted his outburst. "Ah, I'm sorry about that too. I was out of line."

"Don't dodge the question." Her mask of determination slipped as she realized what she had said and tried, unsuccessfully, to stifle a chuckle at the unintentional pun. She composed herself and went on. "There's a lot riding on this, Mr. Dalton. Bela Lugosi is lined up to reprise his role as Boroff. Bela Lugosi! Dracula himself! David Sharpe and Carole Landis have already been signed to play Dodge and Molly. Jack and Bill Witney are ready to start shooting as soon as The Mummy Scourge wraps. So, if there's anything wrong with my story, I need to know what it is before the cameras start rolling."

Dodge took a deep breath and did his best to sound diplomatic. "Well, it's all sort of…" He shrugged. "Unbelievable."

Liz gave another snort of laughter. "Coming from you?"

The barb made him feel a little less diplomatic. "For one thing, it's called 'The Adventures of Dodge Dalton,' not 'The Adventures of Dodge and Molly.' Yet, in the big climax, Molly seems to have center stage." Dodge regretted the comment as soon as he said it, but it was too late to take it back.

Liz, suffused with indignation, seemed to grow a few inches taller. "And what's wrong with that? We need to have a strong, female presence in the story. Today's audiences are far too sophisticated for the hackneyed damsels in distress routine."

"Liz, I—"

"A woman can be every bit as capable as a man. Believe me, I know. I've had to fight against those stereotypes every step of the way. I started out stitching costumes, and now I'm the head writer on a major production." She paused, her demeanor softening as if realizing that she might have gone too far. Her ire dissolved, and she seemed to deflate. "Or I will be. This is my big break, Dodge. Please don't ruin it for me."

Dodge was as stunned by the abrupt reversal as he was by the ferocity of the preceding tirade, though what she was saying was nothing new to him. His friend Nora Holloway had made similar observations. Despite living in the Twentieth Century, it was still tough for a talented female writer to catch a break. "That's not what I meant. Look. I'm sorry. You're right. The story is fine." He shrugged. "It's always a little strange reading about someone who has your name but is nothing like you."

It was almost the truth.

I love you, Dodge.

Molly, the real Molly Rose Shannon, had told him that she loved him just before walking out of his life.

And as if that wasn't bad enough, she'd recently walked back in, not because she loved him or missed him, but because she needed him. Whether or not she did still love him remained an unanswered question, and fear of what that answer might be was the primary reason for his brief escape to the West Coast.

He shook his head. "Anyway, I am sorry about disrupting the set. If you'd like, I'd be happy to apologize to Mr. English."

Liz gave him an appraising glance. "I can't promise that Jack won't have Mop toss you right back out, but why not?"

They had just reached the edge of the set when a scream echoed across the lot.

Dodge glimpsed movement in the corner of his eye, someone falling, hitting the ground with a sickening thud. He turned toward the broken body, then looked up to the lighting boom directly above.

There was another man there, looking down, looking right at Dodge. The man's gaze hardened and he stretched his arms out like wings....

No, not "like" wings. The man had real actual wings extending from his shoulders out several feet past his fingertips in either direction.

The cries of the cast and crew became a low murmur of disbelief, and then a collective gasp as the man tipped forward and fell. An instant before he would have smashed into the body of the fallen rigger, the wings caught the air and the man glided away, skimming just a few feet above the ground, a living arrow aimed right at Dodge.

"Don't these limeys realize that driving on the wrong side of the road will get someone killed," Hurricane Hurley declared jumping onto the curb several seconds ahead of an approaching Alvis Firebird saloon. His languid southern drawl deprived the comment of any sense of urgency that he might have hoped to inject. The driver of the dark-colored touring car tooted his horn as he passed, and motored on down the road, barely slowing.

"You are so funny," Molly Rose Shannon said with a laugh. "As big as you are, there's not much chance of anyone accidentally hitting you. You're about as hard to miss as one of these cathedrals. And you may want to think twice before calling them 'limeys.' We're not likely to get any help from the locals if you insult them."

The big man's eyes followed the departing vehicle. "Limeys."

Molly turned away from the road and let her gaze roam across the vast green lawn to their destination, Trinity College, part of the University of Cambridge. The university and the surrounding city for which it was named, seemed to her like the world's largest collection of churches and cathedrals, and indeed the seven-hundred-year-old institution had begun in an era when ecclesiastical and academic pursuits were indistinguishable from one another. Molly, who had lived most of her life in a rural settlement in the Congo, could have spent hours just wandering through the colleges—or at least those that allowed women—browsing the museums and libraries, but she and Hurricane were not here on a sightseeing tour.

"So where exactly are we meeting with this Wigsteiner fellow?"

"He's lecturing in Nevile's Court," she replied, "although I'm really not sure where that is. And for the last time, it's Wittgenstein, not Wigsteiner."

Hurricane grumbled, then reached out and snared a passing scholar. The student, who up until that moment, had his nose buried in a book, let out a yelp of alarm as he gazed up at the imposing, six-foot, six-inch tall mountain of a man that was Hurricane Hurley. "Which way to Nevile's Court?"

After enduring several seconds of the young man's incoherent stammering, Hurricane cut him off. "Why don't you just take us there?"

"I'm on my way to a class."

"No time to waste, then," Molly remarked with a grin. "Get a move on."

The student stumbled backward, still staring incredulously up at Hurricane, then motioned for them to follow.

The young scholar brought them to a library, where they were subsequently directed to the room where Professor Wittgenstein was holding his lecture. Rather than the expected auditorium with row after row of seats filled with attentive students, the room was actually a small intimate setting, with students gathered haphazardly around their instructor, some on wooden chairs, others sprawled out on the floor. Only a few were taking notes, but it was obvious they were all hanging on the man's every word.

Molly exchanged a look with Hurricane, as they eased into the room, trying not to disrupt the lecture.

Ludwig Wittgenstein was of slight build, and looked almost too young to be a college professor, particularly at an institution as tradition-bound as Cambridge. His dark hair was rumpled and his tweed jacket was badly in need of a steam iron. He moved about the room, rocking back and forth as if to some silent symphony, never looking down. The students seemed to be mesmerized, moving only when it was necessary to get out Wittgenstein's way.

"There is no limit to what man can understand," Wittgenstein said, his eyes raised toward the ceiling, as if in prayer. "Language is the ultimate reality, trumping the bewitchment of all ignorance. It filters out illusion and brings moral perfection. However, when it is forced into a metaphysical environment, into everyday context, it's as if life itself has taken holiday. Frozen, like an ornament on a Christmas tree."

Molly's brow furrowed as she tried to parse what the Professor had just said. Maybe it made more sense in context. Wittgenstein plowed ahead in the same vein for a few moments, then abruptly fell silent, frozen in thought. The students immediately rose and began filing out of the room.

Hurricane grabbed one by the arm. "Where y'all going? He looks like he's thinking of something more to say."

"Believe me, sir, he's finished," the young man replied. "The professor never comes back twice in one lecture."

Hurricane let the student go, shaking his head. "Another absent-minded professor. No wonder Doc Newton recommended him."

Molly shared his frustration. They had come halfway around the world to consult with Wittgenstein, a renowned philosopher and mathematician, only to find a man who seemed barely connected to reality. Of course, given the nature of their problem, maybe that was exactly the sort of help they needed. "Come on, let's go see if we can wake him up."

When the last of students had filed out, Molly moved forward, placed a hand on the man's shoulder and shook him gently to break the trance. "Professor Wittgenstein?"

Wittgenstein blinked and then looked her in the eye. "No, no. I'm done for the day. Make an appointment, young lady."

"We have an appointment, Professor. Findlay Newcombe sent us."

"Findlay?" Wittgenstein blinked again. "Then you must be Miss Shannon." He noticed Hurricane and abruptly took a step back. "Good heavens, you're big."

Hurricane grinned and extended a massive hand. "Pleased to meet you, professor. I'm Hurricane Hurley."

"Hurricane?" Wittgenstein murmured, cocking his head sideways in thought. "No, we're too far north for that."

Molly took him by the arm. "Professor, we need your help with something. Dr. Newcombe says that you're the man to talk to, but I'll warn you, it's going to sound crazy."

"Ha. That's what everyone says about me." He narrowed his gaze, staring into Molly's eyes. "Tell me."

Molly glanced at Hurricane, got an approving nod, and then turned back to Wittgenstein. "I've been having some very strange dreams. Dreams about my dad."

"Your father, I take it, has passed?" He must have caught her pained expression, for he gestured to the exit. "I think better on my feet. Let's take a walk and you can tell me all about these dreams of your father."

Molly's "dad," Nathan Hobbs, was not her father in the biological sense, but he had raised her from a very young age after her parents had died in a disease outbreak. For as long as she had known him, Hobbs had been a Catholic priest operating a mission deep in the African interior on the Congo River, but before that he had led another life as a soldier, serving side-by-side with Hurricane Hurley and Captain Falcon in the Great War and after. Prior to that, he had roamed the earth, studying the mysticism of the Orient and other esoteric religions and philosophies, all in an effort to understand a mysterious prophecy that had haunted him all his life.

Molly had known little and cared less about the past lives of the man she called "dad," until Dodge Dalton had walked into her life. Hobbs, or "the Padre" as Hurricane called him, had joined forces with Dodge to defeat a mysterious villain who possessed what seemed to be supernatural abilities.

During the course of that fight, they had learned a terrible truth—the villain they fought was none other than Captain Falcon himself.

Sort of.

Thousands of years before history began, a scientist—or maybe he was a wizard, the two were hard to separate—had opened a door into what could only be described as another reality, a place like Heaven or Hell, parallel to the reality ordinary humans occupied, but inhabited by strange and powerful entities. The scientist had devised a way to capture those entities in receptacles composed of a mysterious metal known to the ancients as adamantine, much the way that the sorcerers in the Arabian Nights had conjured *djinni* and imprisoned them in lamps and bottles. The adamantine receptacles had functioned like mystical batteries, powering the scientist's many inventions. Little did he realize that the creatures he had enslaved were intent upon escaping back to their reality.

Slowly, insidiously, the entities eroded their master's sanity, capturing his mind even as he had captured them, transforming him into a tool of destruction.

Their escape attempt had unleashed a cataclysm that echoed throughout myth and history—the fall of Atlantis, the Great Flood—but the world of man endured. The survivors of the disaster constructed a prison for the scientist, a sort of limbo where his body wasted away but his twisted consciousness endured for millennia until being inadvertently released by Captain Falcon, whose own mind was subsequently enslaved by "the Prisoner."

With Dodge leading them, she and her dad, and Hurricane too, had eventually thwarted the Prisoner's plan, but that had only been the beginning of their troubles. The source of the Prisoner's power, and his madness, lay at the heart of the prophecy that Father Hobbs sought to understand, for the entities the Prisoner had enslaved still desired their freedom, no matter the cost to the world of mankind. Only one man could stop them, a man ordained by prophecy to be the Child of Skulls, the Lord of Desolation.

Her dad.

To save the world, Father Hobbs had made the ultimate sacrifice, not by dying but rather by choosing to live on the threshold of the door the Prisoner had opened, locked in an eternal struggle with those otherworldly entities, like the little Dutch boy with his finger plugging a hole in the dike, holding back the flood.

Losing him had shaken Molly to the core. She had retreated from the world, from everything associated with mystical prophecies and her father's former life. And from Dodge.

She had believed, perhaps naively, that would be the end of it, and for a time, it was.

Then the dreams had started.

Every night, her father appeared to her and warned her that the Prisoner had returned. At first, she dismissed the visitations as a symptom of grief. Though he wasn't truly dead, he was so removed from her reality that it was very nearly the same thing. But the message was so insistent.

The time is near, he told her. *You must be ready. The prisoner has returned. He will destroy everything.*

And one other thing.

Tell Dodge.

That had been the hardest part. She had left Delhi and journeyed around the world to see the man that she had turned her back on.

Their reunion had gone just about as bad as she expected. They had tried to put their past behind them and focus on the immediate problem, but that was easier said than done. Just being in the same room with him was a very particular sort of Hell, and she knew he felt it too.

Worse, they were no closer to figuring out what the dreams meant.

Their mutual friend, Dr. Findlay Newcombe, sometime-scientific adviser to the President of the United States, had suggested they consult with

Prof. Wittgenstein, but as they were preparing to leave for England, Dodge had gotten the invitation to travel west.

He had accepted, promising to catch up with them in a few days, but Molly wondered if he would keep that promise, or if days would turn into weeks...and into forever.

She would not have blamed him for staying away. She probably deserved that.

She told Wittgenstein most of this—everything but the part about Dodge—as they meandered across the grounds of Trinity College. At first, she was hesitant, anticipating his incredulity, but to her amazement, he not only accepted everything she said, but asked pertinent questions that cut to the heart of the matter.

"And in these dreams, your father warns that the Prisoner has returned," he summarized.

Molly nodded.

Hurricane seemed less enthusiastic. "Professor, you're a man of science. Don't tell me you actually believe all this."

"I am both a philosopher and a mathematician," Wittgenstein replied. "Just like Pythagoras, I believe that mathematics is the language of the universe. But language is the effect, not the cause. In order to have language, we must first presuppose that there exists a world independent of human representation, one which is capable of being conceptualized in terms beyond our ability to quantify."

Hurricane stared at him like he had two heads.

"Think of our reality as the set of numbers between zero and one."

"There ain't no numbers between zero and one."

"No whole numbers, but there are an infinite number of fractions between every number. One half. One quarter. One eighth. On and on, reducing infinitely. That is our reality. We cannot imagine anything outside of it, nothing beyond the absolutes of our existence. Zero and one. Nothing and everything."

Molly nodded uncertainly. "You're saying is that in order to understand reality, we must first admit that it's part of something bigger, something that transcends beyond our ability to understand."

"If that's what he meant," Hurricane replied with a hint of irritation, "I think he would have just said it."

"That's exactly what I meant," Wittgenstein declared. "If what you have told me is true, then it seems likely that your father has reached the edge of our reality. He has not crossed over into the other. Rather, he is caught between ours and the next. He stands at zero, between our reality and it's polar opposite."

"I always thought the opposite of 'real' is 'imaginary,'" Hurricane scoffed.

"Just so." Wittgenstein gave Molly an earnest smile. "And he reaches out to you in a dream."

"I know that my dad is sending me these dreams," Molly replied. "I need to know what he means. The Prisoner is dead. We all saw him die."

Wittgenstein gazed thoughtfully out across the lawn. "Why don't you ask your father?"

"I've tried that. He never answers." She shrugged. "You know how dreams are."

"Hmm. I doubt very much that these are dreams in the ordinary sense. Not that any dream could really be called 'ordinary.' The problem is that we do not have the correct language…" Wittgenstein trailed off, just as he had during the lecture.

"There he goes again," Hurricane muttered. "I'll say this for him. He's definitely the expert on stuff that ain't real."

"Unless I'm very much mistaken," Wittgenstein said, "Those men watching us are quite real."

Hurricane stiffened in embarrassment then followed the professor's gaze. Molly did the same, and spied four men in long black overcoats trying to move inconspicuously across the quad. When the realized that they had been spotted, the men abandoned any pretense of stealth and broke into a run, headed straight for the trio.

"Real enough." Hurricane straightened, rising to his full height and squared off against them, as if intending to meet their charge. "Let's ask 'em what they want."

A sudden breeze snapped at their long coats, revealing the weapons holstered under their arms.

"Hurricane, they've got guns."

"Guns!" Wittgenstein gasped. "Good heavens."

Hurricane's jaw worked as he assessed the situation. Molly knew that he was by no means defenseless. Concealed under his jacket were a pair of custom-made semi-automatic pistols so large and powerful that the recoil would break the wrist of an ordinary man, but Hurricane did not draw them. Instead, he turned to Molly and the professor. "Too many innocent bystanders to let this turn into a shooting match."

"So we run?"

"I reckon. Wigsteiner, you know this place better'n we do. Care to lead the way."

The professor blinked at him for a moment. This was a reality that challenged his comprehension. Molly grabbed his arms and wheeled him around. "Go!"

Hurricane peered down into the grimy old tunnel. "You sure about this, Wigsteiner?"

Moisture leaked from the roof making the footing slippery and dangerous. The passageway smelled musty, and mildew grew on the sides of the concrete walls. Wittgenstein had told them about a network of tunnels that ran beneath the University, connecting the various colleges. He had also started to recount some of the legends and horror stories associated with the tunnels, but Hurricane had cut him off. "Just find one that gets us away from here."

The professor nodded "It comes out at North Paddock, on the other side of the River Cam."

"This tunnel goes underneath the river?" Molly asked.

"That is where the moisture is coming from, Miss Shannon," he replied. "Though, if I'm to be forthright, it really is more of a sewer than a tunnel."

Molly stopped and gazed first at her feet and then up at the roof of the shaft. Hurricane assumed she had issues with close quarters and the fear of being drowned, so he grabbed her by the arm and urged her on silently.

"Who were those men, professor?" Hurricane asked. "Are you in some kind of trouble?"

"Trouble is a relative term, young man," the professor said while keeping up. "I'm afraid all serious scholars are targets these days, from both sides of the shilling interestingly enough."

"Wait a minute, are you telling us those men could be the good guys?" Molly asked.

"Well, possibly, but—"

Suddenly, a bullet hit the roof of the tunnel, harmlessly ricocheting down the shaft. Hurricane pulled the others down and urged them forward, into the tunnel, on their hands and knees. As soon as Molly and the professor passed him, Hurricane hauled out one of his pistols.

"That settles it," he muttered, backing into the dark depths just a few steps behind the others. "They're the bad guys."

At the far end of the tunnel a flashlight came into view, lighting up the shaft and moving in their direction.

A second bullet hit the roof, well off the mark, but it gouged a chunk of concrete from the ceiling. The dribble of water became a stream, pouring from the roof, drenching them with chilly spray.

Hurricane had an idea. "Wigsteiner, how close are we to the end of this tunnel?"

"The ladder to the top is just around the bend, my boy."

"Well what are you waiting for?" Hurricane drew his second custom-made pistol, aimed it and the first at the ceiling and then yelled, "Run!"

As soon as they disappeared around the bend, he pulled the triggers. Deafening explosions, like cannons booming, rocked the enclosed tunnel. The bullets tore open the ceiling and the river poured in like Niagara Falls. Even the mountain-sized Hurricane Hurley could not stand against this torrent.

Water swept past Molly as she braced her back against the metal manhole cover and flexed her legs. This was a task better suited to Hurricane, but since he couldn't be two places at once, it fell to her. The heavy plate groaned in protest, as did the rusted iron ladder rung upon which she stood, but yielded to the steady pressure, rising up enough for her to slide it sideways and let in daylight.

She climbed out of the underground chute and rolled over onto the grass, soaking wet and exhausted from the ordeal. Wittgenstein collapsed alongside her, but for several long seconds, nothing emerged from the manhole except the rushing of waters. Molly rolled over onto her side, a worried frown creasing her face. She edged closer to the opening.

Suddenly, Hurricane burst through the manhole, accompanied by a geyser of water. "No time for a break," he said. "We ain't out of the woods, yet."

He pointed toward the distant campus of Trinity College on the far side of the River Cam. Two cars were racing across the North Avenue Bridge, and judging by their speed and the surly demeanor of the men hanging out the windows, urgently searching the landscape, they were not out for a Sunday drive.

"We can escape into Bin Brook," the professor said. "This way."

"Brook?" Molly looked at Hurricane. "More water?"

Hurricane shrugged and nodded after Wittgenstein's retreating back.

They followed the professor down into a tree-lined creek. The ground was soft, the soil saturated by recent heavy rain and the going was difficult. The normally placid brook now flowed downstream with a brisk authority, the ankle deep water threatening to sweep them off their feet, but the low valley hid them from the line of sight of the searchers.

"We've got to find somewhere to lay low," Hurricane said. "Or better, find a way out of this town without being noticed."

"I have a friend at Magdalene College, a fellow professor of Humanities," the professor said. "A very large fellow, rather like you, Mr. Hurricane. He had a roommate who is also quite large. Honestly, I don't know how two such enormous men can share such a small flat—"

"Wigsteiner! Tick-tock."

"Tick-tock? Oh, of course. Now, I don't have any personal experience here, mind you, but rumor has it that these roommates are quite adept at discreetly bringing..." He glanced at Molly, embarrassment coloring his cheeks. "Ah... female guests...ah...in and out of the university unseen. This fellow owes me a favor, one I have been waiting for the right moment to collect."

"Sounds like now's as good a—"

A tree limb above them cracked and a spray of bark and shredded foliage rained down, accompanied by a thunderous tumult of pistol reports. Hurricane swept Molly and Wittgenstein down with one arm, and then hauled out his pistols and returned fire. Molly could not tell if his shots were finding their targets or if in fact he was even trying to hit their attackers, but for a few seconds, the answering barrage silenced the enemy guns. Evidently, the hunters were not expecting .50 caliber retaliation.

Molly pulled the professor toward the cover of a nearby tree trunk.

"Keep moving," Hurricane urged. "I'm right behind you."

As he laid down a swath of lead in the general direction of the attackers, his guns thundering in two-part harmony—left, right, left, right—Molly followed Wittgenstein down the swiftly flowing brook, splashing water and moving as fast as they could to get away from the attack.

Without any warning, a rather large man jumped out from behind one of the trees. His sudden appearance caused Molly to stumble and she fell face first into the brook. Hurricane wheeled around, aiming his pistols, but Wittgenstein jumped in between him and the new arrival.

"Wait!" he pleaded. "This is the friend I spoke of."

Hurricane stood motionless eying the huge man. He was as tall as Hurricane, and probably weighed over three hundred pounds, with muscles in places no normal person would have them. With his fists clenched and ready-stance, the man looked more like a professional brawler than a Humanities professor.

"What's going on here, Lud?" the man asked, not looking away from Hurley. "I heard shooting. What's wrong? Are you in danger?"

The sound of splashing and voices from further down the brook indicated the pursuers were closing the distance. Wittgenstein helped a thoroughly soaked Molly to her feet. "Yes my boy, I am, but not from these good people. They have been helping me escape. We need a place to…" He glanced at Hurricane. "Lie low."

The huge man looked down at the professor and then at Molly and finally back at Hurricane, obviously debating whether to get involved. Finally, his stern visage cracked with a smile. "Follow me."

He led them up the bank and into a dense copse where they were hidden from view. There, he pulled aside the branches of a large bush to reveal a manhole like the one from which they had just emerged. The cover was already askew.

Molly groaned. "Another sewer tunnel?"

The big man ignored her and turned his attention to Hurricane. "I'm afraid it's going to be a tight squeeze for you, but if I can do it, so can you."

"Another sewer tunnel? " Molly repeated. "Don't tell me this one goes underneath the river as well?"

"It doesn't, now hurry up."

Wittgenstein lowered himself into the hole, followed by Molly and Hurricane. Their savior however remained outside. "Follow the tunnel, Lud," he whispered. "I'll meet you along the way."

Then, without another word, he slid the manhole cover into place, sealing them in the darkness.

Molly listened intently as she descended into the darkness, but the expected noise of battle did not occur. Wittgenstein's big friend had evidently slipped away unnoticed, and the men chasing them had not discovered the hidden manhole. Her sense of trepidation diminished further when she reached the foot of the ladder and discovered the floor underfoot to be surprisingly dry, and free of the expected foul odors. This sewer had not been active in years, and now served only as a means to discreetly facilitate indiscreet activities.

Despite the darkness, they navigated the sewer tunnel with ease, and before long, a light appeared in the distance, drawing them onward. It was Wittgenstein's friend, who had evidently hastened back to the other end of the tunnel in order to guide them onward. He offered no comment, but merely waved them along. When they reached the end of the line, the man reached up and pulled down a folding ladder. As the ladder came down, a spring-loaded mechanism simultaneously opened a trap door overhead.

A few minutes later, the bedraggled group was gathered in an elegant, if cluttered, library that looked like it could have been used for a stage production of a Sherlock Holmes story. Their savior had been joined by another enormous man who, although smiling, did not look pleased by the intrusion.

"Thank you for bringing us here, my friend," Wittgenstein said. "I am pleased that the rumors of your secret entrance were not unfounded."

"Of course, Lud," the man replied. "Though it won't remain a secret if you tell everyone about it."

"Secret?" Hurricane snorted. "Sounds like it's already the talk of the town."

"Rumors that we start in order to hide the truth. The real purpose of the tunnel is part of Her Majesty's effort to prepare for the coming war."

"A war that is closer than most realized," added the other man. "Those men looking for you are German agents. Nazis."

This revelation stunned Molly. She recalled the earlier abbreviated discussion about good guys and bad guys, but now she finally understood what it meant. England was bracing for another war with Germany, and given the technological advances made in the all-too-brief post-war lull, if or when that war came, it would make the Great War pale into insignificance.

"Why are the Nazis after you?"

Wittgenstein ignored Molly's pointed question. "You have our word that we will not reveal its location or purpose to a soul."

"If you can get us out of here," Hurricane intoned, "I'm ready to forget everything about this place."

Their hosts exchanged a glance and then Wittgenstein's friend nodded. "I think we can help speed you on your way."

Dodge pushed Liz out of the way, inadvertently sending her crashing into the craft services table, unleashing a blizzard of fruit and stale pastries. It could have been a scene from a Keystone Kops film, but Dodge wasn't laughing.

Even as Liz careened toward the food table, Dodge dropped into a squat and rolled onto his back. The flying man cut through the air, mere inches above him, so close that the tips of his wings brushed the ground behind him, leaving a trail of friction sparks.

Metal. Like knives grinding against stone. And headed right for me.

Even as the thought flashed through Dodge's head, he struck out with his feet, catching the man in the chest and deflecting him off his intended flight path. The kick wasn't very powerful, but it was enough to send the man cartwheeling away, the feather-blades whooshing past, so close that one of Dodge's sleeves suddenly fell open, sliced apart by a razor-sharp edge. Just when it seemed that the man would crash into the wall, the wings spread wide, and the man effortlessly began ascending, swooping back up into the sky.

Dodge stared up at the receding figure in disbelief. This was not the first time he had encountered men with the ability to fly, and then as now, people were in mortal danger, though in truth, this man seemed to be gliding rather than truly flying. The bird-like wings were reminiscent of the Hawkmen from the Flash Gordon serials, but unlike the props used in those productions, these wings were not only functional but evidently deadly. The flying man's head darted this way and that, as if trying to decide what to do next, then his gaze locked onto Dodge and he lined up for another attack.

Dodge raced over to the stunned Liz and pulled her behind the overturned table. A moment later, a chunk of the table disappeared, neatly excised by a wing-blade. Dodge waited a beat then looked over the top of the barrier, just in time to see the flying man rising once more into the sky.

Dodge turned to Liz. "Are you alright?"

The screenwriter brushed the food scraps from her dress and attempted to straighten her mussed up hair. "What just happened?"

Nearby, a cluster of crew and actors, some in Black Legion attire some in mummy wrappings and ghoulish make-up gathered around the unfortunate victim. Someone cried out for an ambulance, and someone else countered with a request for the police.

Dodge stared up at the silhouette of the flying killer who was turning a lazy circle a good two hundred feet overhead, biding his time until another chance to pounce on his target presented itself. There was little question in Dodge's mind that he was that target, but the killer had not shown the slightest hesitation about hurting innocent people.

"I need to get away from here," he said, thinking aloud. "As far from all these people as I can."

Without waiting for a reply, he grabbed a corner of the overturned table and launched himself into motion.

"Dodge! Wait!"

Ignoring Liz's cry of protest, he made a beeline for Jack English's Packard convertible and dove beneath it just as the birdman sliced through the air where he had been a moment before.

"Whew, that was close!"

Dodge's eyes widened in surprise at the sound of Liz's voice. Somehow, the woman had managed to slip under the car beside him. He shook his head in dismay. "You need to get away from here," he said. "Away from me."

"And miss out on a real Dodge Dalton adventure? Think again, buster."

Dodge sensed that further argument would be pointless. "Fine. You can help me find my way around this place." He squirmed forward to make sure that the birdman wasn't perched on the car, waiting to take his head off.

"Find your way… What?"

"Move it!" Dodge said as he crawled out and sprang to his feet, then immediately clambered over the sideboard and into the driver's seat of the Packard.

He had just succeeded in coaxing the throaty eight-cylinder engine to life when Liz's voice commanded his attention once more. "This is Jack's car. You can't—"

"Get in or get left," he barked. He looked skyward again and found the winged killer, circling high above like a hawk eyeing a rabbit in a field, perhaps contemplating how best to deal with his prey now that Dodge was ensconced in the vehicle.

Without waiting for Liz to make up her mind, Dodge let out the clutch and stomped down on the gas pedal. As the car lurched forward, Liz hopped onto the running board and then threw herself over the side, falling head first into the footwell.

Like a time-machine, the Packard hurtled forward and into the past, specifically, into turn-of-the-century Mexico. A full-scale colonial hacienda appeared before him, replete with fake cactuses, real horses, and dozens of hapless extras in full period costume moving about the plaza. Dodge laid on the horn, which had the effect of triggering a stampede that only further blocked the way.

He tilted the rear view mirror skyward so he could keep one eye on what lay ahead and one on the assassin above. "Molly, which way?"

His passenger righted herself. "Liz."

"What?"

"Jack's going to kill me for this," she muttered and pointed to the gap between the stucco facades. "Through there."

Dodge slewed the Packard through the plaza and abruptly emerged in what looked like Dodge City, circa 1876. More horses blocked his way, some ridden by men in full western regalia, others hitched to carts and wagons. Dodge honked repeatedly, but was forced to gear down and advance at a crawl as animals and actors grudgingly gave ground.

He started at the sound of a gunshot, but when it was followed by another, and then several more, he realized that the reports were merely the sound of the actors firing off the blanks in their prop guns, answering his honks with some noise of their own making. The air in front of him grew thick with gunsmoke, but then a different sound punctuated the tumult and a large gray divot appeared on the Packard's motor cowling, just a few inches beyond the windshield.

That was a real bullet, Dodge thought. He looked skyward and saw the birdman killer swooping past, just fifty feet overhead, the pistol in the man's right hand tiny with the distance but nonetheless unmistakable. The flying man banked and then immediately swooped toward the Packard, the gun belching fire repeatedly.

Bullets smashed into the hood, ricocheting away over the heads of the milling actors who at last seemed to grasp that there was a more serious threat than the disruption caused by the errant vehicle. They scattered for the relative safety of the rickety boardwalk fronting the mock Old West buildings, giving Dodge the opening he needed. He punched the gas pedal once more, and was rewarded with a shuddering lurch and an eruption of black smoke that billowed out from under the hood.

A bullet punched into the seat between him and Liz. Another struck the back seat. The Packard gave another tortured shudder and then ground to a stop, the smoke now forming a column of Biblical proportions.

"Out!" Dodge ordered.

He clambered over the sideboard but this time he waited for Liz to catch up. Like it or not, she had thrown her lot in with him and that made her safety his responsibility. He was also counting on her to guide him through the anachronistic maze of the Republic back lot, though he was beginning to believe that running away was no longer a tenable strategy. He turned a slow circle, taking in the length and breadth of the Western set. He and Liz could hide in one of the wooden structures. That would deprive the killer of a target, at least temporarily, but there was no telling what the man would do then.

I need to go on the offensive, he thought. *But how can I fight someone I can't reach.*

He was surrounded by men with guns—six-shooters, rifles, shotguns—all of them movie props, loaded with blanks. Useless. Then he spotted something familiar in the distance, the stone battlements of a medieval castle.

"Molly, this way!"

"Liz!" she shouted again, and this time Dodge realized what he had done.

"Sorry. Liz, get us to that castle."

She seemed to grasp what he was asking and grabbed hold of his elbow. She steered him down the dusty Wild West street, dodging piles of horse manure, and into a short alley that opened up on what looked like an idyllic but utterly abandoned New England neighborhood.

"Not shooting here today," Liz said, panting as they sprinted down the street. As if to prove her wrong, bullets began raining down from the sky, pockmarking the pavement beside them.

The crenelated battlements of the castle were barely visibly, peeking over the tops of the ersatz Cape Cod houses, and Dodge veered in that direction, darting down a narrow alley that seemed more an access trail than part of the set, and emerged a moment later in the castle courtyard, and right in the middle of a swashbuckler adventure film.

"Cut!" The director leaped from his chair and began stalking toward Dodge and Liz. His face was purple with rage and looked as if it could explode, and seconds later it nearly did when bullets began tearing into the straw littered ground at his feet.

Screams from the actors and crewmembers echoed inside the opened set. Another fusillade of bullets swept the area, blasting enormous holes in the walls, which Dodge now realized were nothing but wood, plastered and painted to resemble the sturdy stone of a 14th Century Norman fortification.

So much for the promise of a bulletproof refuge, Dodge thought. But he spotted something else that gave him hope.

Crouching down behind a bale of hay was a man wearing a bright red outfit, complete with a matching peaked hat and a jaunty feather. There was quiver full of arrows slung across his back, and in his hands was an ornately carved bow of white wood.

Dodge scrambled over to the cowering actor and pointed at the bow. "Is that real?"

The man gaped at him, a strange haughty look replacing his earlier terror. "Of course it is. Cheap props are for the extras."

Several shots rang out and hit the walls above them, sending shards of plaster and debris down onto their location.

"Good," Dodge said grabbing the bow and snatching a handful of arrows from the quiver.

The actor let out an indignant yelp, but Dodge ignored him, nocking an arrow and rolling over to locate the soaring hawkman. He pulled the string back, feeling the tension as the wooden bow bent. He had never shot a bow and arrow and wasn't sure what would happen when he let go, but he was determined to be more than just a helpless victim.

The hawkman soared above firing randomly into the midst of the set, probably trying to stir up pandemonium and flush out his prey. Dodge tracked him with the blunt tip of the arrow, leading him by a few feet, and then when he felt the timing was right, loosed the projectile.

The bowstring raked Dodge's left forearm painfully, skewing his aim even as the bow shuddered in his hand with the release of the stored torsion energy. The bow fell from his nerveless fingers and the arrow flew harmlessly past the hawkman, but the shot was not entirely without effect. The assassin spotted the missile and banked away reflexively, colliding with a large decorative banner that hung from a flagpole mounted to the battlements. Entangled in the fabric like a fly in a spider's web, the assassin struggled for a moment and then collapsed straight down, crashing to straw-covered ground twenty feet from Dodge's position.

Dodge scooped up the bow in his right hand and charged the killer who was still partially shrouded in the banner. A gun materialized from the tangle but Dodge did not slow. Instead, he swung the weapon like a baseball bat, swatting the extended hand. The wood splintered with the impact, sending a painful jolt up Dodge's forearm, but the pistol went flying.

With the hawkman at last grounded and weaponless, Dodge felt a glimmer of hope. *Now at least it will be a fair fight,* he thought. But a moment later, a pair of silvery wings, at least fifteen feet from tip to tip, unfurled and the fabric entangling the man fell away in shreds, giving Dodge his first good look at the man who was trying to kill him.

He was just a man, though his skin-tight aerodynamic black bodysuit, replete with a hood and goggles to cover his face, revealed little about his appearance. In any event, there was no time to study the details. The man was already moving toward Dodge, swiping his wings back and forth in front of him with dizzying speed.

Dodge recalled how the razor-sharp "feathers" had sliced through the wooden table earlier and knew they would do the same to his flesh if they made contact. He scrambled backwards, slipping in the straw, retreating mere inches away from the whirling fans of death.

"Here!"

Liz's shout could not have come at a more inopportune moment, but from the corner of his eye, he saw a large disc soaring through the air toward him. It was a decorative shield, one of several that had been hanging on the castle wall. Before Dodge could even think about trying to catch the piece of armor, a bladed-wing slashed it out of the air, slicing it neatly in two.

The distraction gave Dodge the opening he so desperately needed. He levered himself off the ground and threw a right jab that connected with the assassin's jaw, knocking the man backward. The wings flailed out, giving Dodge a chance to land another blow, a gut punch that staggered the assassin and put him on his back.

A cry of pain tore from the man's lips as he landed hard on the apparatus to which the wings were attached. He struggled to right himself, but now the device which had given him the power of unlimited movement in three dimensions had rendered him as helpless as an overturned turtle.

Dodge started toward the man, vaguely aware of the crowd that was now gathering around them—actors, extras and crew—eager to see an old-fashioned brawl of the kind they merely simulated with props and carefully choreographed stunt work. Dodge however, had already had his fill of violence.

"It's over," he told the man. "Your wings are clipped. Give up."

The man sneered at him, then spat a gob of blood onto the straw. He twisted his head back and forth, as if to crack cartilage from within his neck, then brought his hands to his chest, punching the silver clasp where the straps of his wing apparatus joined over his heart. The straps fell away, freeing the man to roll sideways, away from the wings that had been an impediment just a moment before. In a flash, he was back on his feet, fists raised and to all appearances, ready to give Dodge the knock-down drag-out fight that the crowd was so eager for.

The man's fists were not empty however. Each hand was curled around what looked like the grip of a pistol, albeit without the rest of the weapon.

He twisted his hands outward, and strips of silver metal, the same material as the wings, burst forth, encircling his hands in what looked like protective metal gauntlets.

A low murmur of apprehension rolled through the crowd. Dodge assumed a pugilistic stance, but knew it would take more than his limited boxing skills to best this foe. Without hesitation, the killer took a step forward and lashed out with one armored hand. Dodge dried to duck away, but the fist scored a glancing blow that sent Dodge reeling into the crowd.

He expected the assembled group to scatter, but to his astonishment, they caught him and kept him on his feet. One man, wearing what looked like a chainmail halberd and a bright red tunic, thrust something in front of him. "Here. Use this."

It was a broadsword. Except, when Dodge wrapped his hand around the hilt, he realized it was far too lightweight to be an actual metal blade.

Another prop.

The wooden blade wouldn't be much good against the metal fists of his foe, but he was nonetheless grateful for the assistance. And maybe his opponent wouldn't realize it was fake.

He advanced, raising the sword in a two-handed grip and charged. The man raised his gauntlets to ward off what he thought would be an overhead hacking blow, but at the last instant, Dodge dropped the blade low and stabbed it into the man's exposed midriff. If it had been an actual steel sword, he would have been unable to execute such a quick reversal, but the lightweight prop posed no such difficulty. Unfortunately, its lack of heft also reduced the effectiveness of the thrust. Instead of skewering the killer, the blunt wooden blade hit the man with all the force of a broom handle; enough to take the wind out of his sails, but not nearly enough to kill him.

Nevertheless, the jab doubled the man over like a worm on a fishhook. Dodge drew back quickly, raised the blade overhead and this time it was no feint. He brought the prop sword down on the man's head with such force that the sturdy wooden blade splintered like a piece of balsa wood. The assassin went to his knees, then pitched forward, unconscious in the middle of the courtyard.

The crowd cheered as if they had witnessed the epic prizefight of the century. Knights and medieval peasants, cowboys and even a few men in Black Legion and mummy costumes—gathered around Dodge, pounding him on the back in hearty congratulations.

The celebration was short lived however. A cry of alarm rippled through the group and Dodge saw several hands pointing to the sky where several shapes that looked like vultures were circling.

Dodge knew they weren't birds.

As if on cue, the formation shifted and two of the winged men angled toward the ground.

"Run!" The crowd dispersed, disappearing into the mock-castle, diving under hay wains, taking shelter wherever they could, leaving Dodge standing alone in the middle of the courtyard.

He looked around frantically for something he could use to defend himself. It had taken everything he had to defeat just one. There was no way he could take on a whole flock of them.

Then he spotted the first killer's wings, discarded and forgotten a few steps from where the unconscious man lay. Dodge knew he could not hope to master the apparatus in the brief seconds before the next attack began, but the razor sharp metal feathers were a far better weapon than anything he might find on the Republic studios backlot. He gripped the straps and hefted the wings up, holding them in front of him, ready to slash them back and forth.

The hawkmen however paid him no heed. Instead, they swooped down, and without ever touching the ground, scooped up their fallen comrade and bore him back into the sky. A third flyer came in on their heels, grabbing the wing apparatus with similar ease.

Dodge watched as they rejoined the others high above, and then the entire formation moved off, heading west. Soon, they were nothing but specks in the bright blue sky. Then, they weren't there at all.

"What the hell were those things?" one of the crewmembers asked.

"I wish I knew," Dodge muttered.

He became aware of Liz standing in front of him. "What the heck were those things?"

Dodge thought about the wings, how lightweight and indestructible they had seemed to be. He was no expert, he was pretty sure he recognized the silvery metal from which they had been crafted.

Adamantine.

"I don't know," he admitted, "but I do know someone who might be able to help us figure it out."

The grains of silvery metal began to shake and shift, like sand about to slide down the neck of an hour glass. After a few seconds, a distinctive pattern of ripples began to appear as the grains organized into concentric rings that perfectly matched the frequency of the sound waves—inaudible to the human ear—that were bombarding the test chamber. Dr. Findlay Newcombe jotted a few observations in a notebook and then made an adjustment to the tone generator. The metal grains responded by reorganizing into complex geometric patterns known as Chladni figures.

"Ah," Newcombe muttered, "Now we're getting somewhere."

The ringing of the telephone startled him, causing him to drop both pencil and notebook. He scooped them up, and then jumped again as the insistent bell repeated its alarm. He scooped up the receiver, awkwardly since he had forgotten to put down the notebook first, and held it up. "I'm in the middle an experiment. Can't this wait?"

A female voice, scratchy with static, filled his ear. *"Please stand-by for long-distance from Hollywood, a Mr. David Dalton calling."*

His irritability evaporated. "Dodge, is that you?" He shouted into the phone. "How is Hollywood? Have you met Greta Garbo, yet?"

"Not yet, Doc, but the place is crawling with movie starlets, so I imagine it's just a matter of time."

"Give her my regards when you do."

"I will, but that's not the reason I called."

There was a momentary pause, filled only with the crackle of random electrical bursts. "Dodge, are you still there?"

"Something happened today. I'm not sure how much I should say over the phone, but you'll probably read about it in the papers, so I'll just share the highlights. I was attacked by men with...well, wings."

"Like airplanes?"

"No. Like hawks. Actual wings strapped to their backs. Needless to say, the episode did not unfold without some casualties, and quite a mess to the studio, so I imagine you'll be reading about all the chaos associated with that. It all seems a bit familiar, if you take my meaning."

"I do." He did. His friendship with Dodge had begun following a similar incident.

"I got a pretty good look at one of them. I don't know what makes them tick, but I can tell you that the wings they were using are made out of our favorite substance...or at least I'm pretty sure that it's ...well, you know."

Newcombe allowed the revelation to sink in. Dodge could only be referring to adamantine, the very substance Newcombe was investigating presently.

Adamantine was the rarest, most mysterious element Newcombe had ever encountered, so indestructible that it had proved, thus far, impossible to melt or refine the ore. The ancient entity whom Dodge had taken to calling "the Prisoner" had, through means as yet unknown, solved that problem and in so doing, fully exploited the properties of adamantine to create weapons of indescribable power, but those ancient devices had gone dormant following Father Hobbs sacrifice in India.

Had someone else had cracked the mystery of forging adamantine? Or somehow tapped into that ancient source of power?

"Dodge, if you're right, then you may be facing a very dangerous enemy. The ability to fly may only be the tip of the iceberg."

"I'm aware of that. That's why I'm calling. I'm working with the police and we've got a plan to draw these killers out into the open, but we're shooting in the dark. We need to know who…or what we're dealing with."

"Ada…" He stopped himself. "The metal is rare, but it's still a naturally occurring substance, so it's not impossible that someone else had been conduction similar research. Walter Barron may have shared his knowledge before…" He stopped himself again. *No need to take a trip down memory lane.* "The problem has never been finding the ore, but rather casting it and unlocking its unique properties. All of the machines from the Outpost stopped working when—"

"I know," Dodge said quickly, cutting him off. *"But is it possible that we missed something? Is there another way to use this stuff that we've missed?"*

"Anything is possible."

There was a long silence on the line. *"Doc. I want you to come out West as soon as you can."*

Newcombe felt a twinge of apprehension. "You want me to come out there?"

Every time Dodge pulled him out of the laboratory, away from his experiments, it always led to big trouble. *Of course,* he thought wistfully, *it also sometimes leads to good things, too.*

"I have a feeling this is going to get a lot worse. I think you're right. We've only seen the tip of the iceberg."

"I'll come as soon as I can," He promised. "Try not to do anything reckless until I get there." He replaced the receiver and absentmindedly stared off into space.

Men with adamantine wings in California? How was it possible?

A knock at the door startled him. It opened to reveal the familiar face of a young man, attired in the uniform of a Massachusetts Institute of Technology campus policeman. "Someone topside to see you, doc."

First the phone call and now this. How am I ever going to get any work done?

"I'm not expecting company, Cecil." A glance at the wall clock revealed that it was already well past seven p.m. He had missed dinner again.

"The man said to give you this." Cecil took a step into the room, careful not to violate the protocols established to protect Newcombe's research, and held out a card. Newcombe approached and took the card, after which Cecil promptly retreated to the other side of the doorway.

"Professor Padraig Dunn, University of Cairo," Newcombe muttered. "I didn't know Cairo even had a..." He looked up sharply and then a grin spread across his face. Dunn? Fiona? He turned to Cecil again. "This Professor Dunn, was he alone?"

"No. Has another fella with him. Colored fella."

Behind his large spectacles, Newcombe's face creased in dismay, his moment of joy slipping away. "Please show them down."

"Doc, you know better'n that. The lab is off limits, even to me."

"Yes, yes. Of course, Cecil. You are absolutely correct. I'll come up. Hold on a moment."

Newcombe went over to an open safe, placed the notebook inside, and closed it securely. He then pulled on his tweed coat and followed the policeman to the elevator that would take them more than two hundred feet up to the MIT campus.

The elevator opened inside an obscure building on Albany Street. The structure was designated as a test facility for electrical research, and as far as anyone knew, that was what it was. Underneath was a much different story, however. Far below the college campus, Dr. Findlay Newcombe's new top-secret government laboratory conducted research vital to the nation's security.

Newcombe's career had oscillated like an electrical current, rising, falling and rising again. After his friend Dodge Dalton thwarted a diabolical plan by industrialist Walter Barron, Newcombe had been invited back to government service—invited was perhaps too polite a term. More like drafted—to conduct research on the strange metal. Adamantine promised to be a revolutionary substance if Newcombe could figure out how to utilize it.

Newcombe followed Cecil to the lobby of the Albany Street building where two men waited—one an older man with wild white hair that Newcombe assumed could only be Padraig Dunn, and a wiry, weathered dark-skinned man in a simple business suit who held a cracked leather valise in one hand. Dunn might have borne a passing resemblance to Fiona, but it was hard to tell; his face was puffy with bruises and several sutured lacerations, as if he had recently been in an accident...or a fight. Both men appeared anxious, a condition that did not improve as they spotted Newcombe.

"Are you Dr. Findlay Newcome?" Dunn said, skipping any sort of formal invitation. There was just a hint of Irish brogue in his speech.

"I am. And you must be Professor Dunn. Forgive me for being direct, but are you related to Fiona Dunn?"

Both of the visitors winced as if the name evoked a painful memory, but Dunn answered. "She's my daughter. She told me all about you, Dr. Newcombe. That's why I'm here."

Something clicked in Newcombe's brain. "Is she all right? Has something happened?"

The two men looked at each other. "It would be best to discuss this in private."

Newcombe felt his heart begin to race. Something *had* happened to Fiona.

He found himself thinking about the delightful young archaeologist who had assisted him and Dodge in their effort to stop Walter Barron. The thought that she had come to harm was unbearable. He led the men to an unused office and firmly closed the door behind them.

Dunn did not immediately address the looming issue. "This is Sadiki, my faithful servant and friend."

Newcombe extending his hand to the dark-skinned man who seemed surprised by the gesture, but accepted the handclasp.

"Now," Newcombe said, "you must tell me. Is Fiona all right?"

Dunn sighed. "I wish that I could answer that question, but the awful truth is that I simply do not know. Fiona is missing."

"I'll help you find her," Newcombe said, without hesitation.

"I fear it's not going to be as simple as that." Dunn turned to Sadiki. "Show him."

Sadiki opened the valise and took out a silver-colored object that looked to Newcombe like a piece from a chess set, a rook but topped with four horizontal disks, like stacked hats, and adorned with strange hieroglyphic symbols.

"This is a djed amulet," Dunn said. "Often associated with Ptah, the Egyptian creator god, and Osiris, the god of the afterlife. The djed is a symbol of stability. Victory over death in the afterlife. This one however, is unique."

He took the amulet from Sadiki and handed it to Newcombe. The djed pillar was unexpectedly light in Newcombe's hand, and cool to the touch. "Is this aluminum?"

"I think you know what it is, Dr. Newcombe."

"Adamantine," Newcombe whispered, astonished, especially after Dodge's call. "But that's impossible."

"I'm sure there are tests you could perform that would confirm it."

"You don't understand. Adamantine is the hardest substance known to man. Harder than diamond. It cannot be melted by any modern process. I take it you found this in Egypt?"

Dunn glanced at Sadiki again but did not answer.

"The Egyptians may have done some marvelous things, but they certainly were not capable of refining and casting adamantine."

"Yet, there it is."

Newcombe gripped the amulet. "How does this pertain to Fiona's disappearance?"

"To explain that, I must begin at the beginning, but our time is short. Sadiki and I have booked passage on the Queen Mary, leaving for Southampton tomorrow. From there, we will continue on to Egypt to…" He sighed and took a breath. "Begin the search for my daughter. Will you help us?"

Newcombe wondered about the coincidence of Dodge's call and his agreement to fly out to California to meet with him, but the only thing he could think was that Fiona was in trouble, and he had to find her.

California would have to wait.

CHAPTER 5— DARK WATERS

Although it was late summer, the breeze off the North Sea sent a chill through Molly Rose Shannon, as she, Hurricane Hurley, and Professor Wittgenstein crouched in the shadows behind St. John's Church, watching the roads and biding their time. Their arrival in Clacton-on-Sea, a resort town located on the Tendring peninsula in the county of Essex, had not gone unnoticed it seemed, and their plan to borrow a boat from an acquaintance of Wittgenstein, and travel south to the mouth of the river Thames, and eventually into London, their final destination, had stalled.

Another car full of tough-looking men—the third they had seen—sped by. Strangers were common in the holiday town, but the stern-looking Nazi agents stuck out like a sore thumb amid the frolicking vacationers. Unfortunately, Hurley was even more conspicuous, which necessitated remaining in the shadows.

The car sped around a corner and disappeared down the road, but Molly knew it would be back, or another like it. The Nazis were quickly setting a noose around them, cutting off their planned escape route.

Molly's thoughts kept drifting to Dodge. Not because she missed him—she kept telling herself that—but because his presence would have evened those odds a little. As imposing as Hurricane Hurley was, Dodge had a way of doing the impossible.

But Dodge wasn't here. He had chosen a different path.

She pushed him back out of her thoughts.

The pier, where the promised boat was supposed to be moored, was lined with dozens of shops and carnival attractions, all brightly lit against the descending twilight, sparkling like a gem encrusted finger, pointing out into the inky blackness of the North Sea. Less than a mile separated them from that goal, but it might has well have been a hundred miles. There was only one road leading onto the pier, and Molly felt certain it was being watched carefully.

Only one road, she thought. A sick feeling settled into her gut as she realized there was one other route open to them. She turned to the others, and had to force the words past the lump in her throat. "There's no way to reach the pier unnoticed by land. The only way to get there is by water."

Hurricane's facial expression said what his mouth did not. He obviously did not like where this was headed.

"They aren't watching the water," she added, helplessly.

"I am an excellent swimmer if that's what you're worried about," Wittgenstein declared in a tone probably meant to sound reassuring. He used his hands to wipe the dirt off the cuff of his trousers. He then turned and faced the water off in the distance. "Looks like all those laps at the pool are about to pay off. And you're absolutely correct. Nobody would ever think to look for us out on the water."

"We'd freeze in seconds," Hurricane said. "But maybe we can skirt along the beach."

It was a desperate plan and if they were detected, they would almost literally be caught between the devil and the deep, but it was the best option on a short list of bad options.

Molly held her breath, listening intently as the crunch-crunch sound grew louder…closer still, and then stopped. She slowly rose up and peeked over the wall. A man stood, unmoving, not a stone's throw from where they hid. For nearly a full minute he did not move. Then, he shook his hand impatiently, and Molly realized that he was holding a leash in that hand.

Just walking his dog, Molly thought, letting her breath out in a quiet sigh.

His business done, the dog trotted away and the man walked after him.

The man continued down the street in the opposite direction. Before he was gone however, another man appeared at the end of the street, him, only this time it was not so obvious what his intention was. Molly lowered herself back into the shadows as the crunch of the second man's footsteps grew louder, then diminished to nothing.

"We need to go," she whispered. "Right now."

Hurricane nodded reluctantly, and then led the way, walking stooped over until they were well away from the street lights near the church, whereupon he stood up and began running. They sprinted through the yard of a village home and continued down the slope toward the shore. A rickety old gate rose up before them. Hurricane opened it a little too vigorously, and a tortured metallic shriek filled the air. The noise startled a herd of goats grazing on the other side of the fence. As the animals scurried away, their bleats and the bells hung around their necks sounded like the clamor of a fire alarm.

They reached the water's edge a few seconds later bore left, heading toward the pier. Errant waves and splashed their ankles, chilling Molly, but they didn't slow.

Behind them, flashlight beams reaching out to probe the shoreline, searching the sand and the sea beyond. Searching for them.

Hurricane grasped Molly's arm and pointed to a dark lump on the sand directly ahead, a small rowboat, inexplicably abandoned on the beach. She had somehow caught a glimpse of it illuminated by a house light, a stroke of luck no doubt.

"That's a bit of luck," Professor Wittgenstein said.

"I don't believe in luck, Professor," Hurricane said, heaving the boat out into the surf. "But I'll take it when I can get it. All aboard."

They clambered in and with another shove, Hurricane freed the boat from the sucking sand underneath and drove it out until the surf was up to his thighs before he too climbed over the gunwale and deployed the oars.

A flurry of flashlight beams raced down the shoreline, illuminating the surface of the water searching for them. Voices echoed in the night air, the language unfamiliar, but shouts and commands easy enough to interpret.

Hurricane began to row with powerful strokes, trying to put as much distance as he could between them and the shoreline

"What if they see us?" Molly whispered.

"I'm rowing as fast as I can," Hurricane replied between breaths.

"Luck breaks our way again," Wittgenstein said. "Look!"

Molly followed his pointing finger. Between them and the lights of the pier, the silvery smear of a fog bank hovered above the water.

"They'll never find us in that."

"And we might row halfway to Belgium if we lose our bearings," Hurricane replied, but nevertheless angled the boat toward the heavy cloud.

The mist enveloped them like a damp blanket, growing thicker and heavier the deeper they went. Molly understood now why people compared it to pea soup. She felt as if she was suffocating.

Hurricane stopped rowing and lifted the oars out of the water, allowing the vessel to drift. The boat rocked gently, an invisible surface current pushing them along. The shouts on the shoreline were growing faint, but whether the boat was getting closer to the pier, or being dragged out to sea, it was impossible to say.

Suddenly, the boat hit a solid object with a loud clank. The current whipped the bow around and it struck again, and then they were scraping against it—whatever it was—with a shrill screech.

More voices now, not from the shore but above them, echoing in the fog. Other sounds, too. Footsteps tapping on a metal surface, and the distinctive mechanical sound of guns being cocked.

A brilliant light shone down on them, illuminating the fog like a solid column of pure white. The glow revealed a metal tower, rising up before them, and painted on its dark surface were the numbers 4 and 8, and a strange symbol—an oval-shaped wreath of laurel leaves, and inside it, an eagle perched atop a swastika.

"A German U-boat," Hurricane snarled. "This is why I don't believe in luck."

Dodge Dalton and Liz Sansom stood on platform B at Union Station waiting as porters loaded their luggage into the baggage car. They were surrounded by families and business travelers gathered to say their good-byes. Further down the platform, Dodge saw Inspector Thomas Gwinn, the man in charge of the investigation into the attack at the studio. Gwinn wore a sharp gray suit, and was accompanied by two similarly attired men, whom Dodge assumed were plainclothes officers from the Los Angeles Police Department. The trio were trying to blend in with the other passengers, but the six-foot tall, broadly built senior detective would have had trouble blending in anywhere. It was not Gwinn's size however, but rather his suspicious demeanor that gave him away. Subtlety was evidently not a highly-prized skill for the men of the LAPD.

Though their acquaintance could be measured in hours, Dodge had taken an instant liking to Gwinn, probably because the inspector reminded him of Hurricane Hurley. Dodge was acutely aware of his friend's absence, particularly in the aftermath of the attack at the studio backlot.

Hurricane would have made short work of the hawkman, no doubt about that.

Or he might have gotten himself killed.

Dodge shook his head to banish the thought. Hurricane Hurley was invincible; of that he had no doubt.

But, invincible or not, Hurricane wasn't here.

There was just him, dangling himself out in the open like bait for the winged killers, while Gwinn and the two plainclothes policemen waited to close the trap.

It had been Dodge's idea to use himself to lure the killers into the open, but Gwinn, desperate to close the books on the bizarre attack, which had cost one man his life and thousands of dollars of damage to the Republic Pictures studio, had been the one to suggest making a very high-profile jaunt to Palm Springs. Since Dodge had clearly been the target of the winged assassin, it was only a matter of time before a second attempt was made, but this time, the battlefield would be a place of their choosing, well away from the densely populated city, where innocents might get caught in the crossfire.

A boy carrying a stack of newspapers wandered the platform, shouting out the headline that graced the cover of the evening edition of The Los Angeles Times.

"DODGE DALTON THWARTS KILLERS IN REAL LIFE ADVENTURE AT REPUBLIC STUDIOS."

The headline was not nearly as important as the story below the fold, which revealed Dodge's intention to travel east to Palm Springs, where he would meet with his longtime associate, presidential science adviser Findlay Newcombe, to discuss the mysterious wing apparatus worn by the would-be assassin. It would not take a genius to figure out that Dodge intended to travel to Palm Springs by train. If all went according to plan, the killers would head there as well, perhaps riding on the same train or possibly traveling ahead by car, and make their move shortly after Dodge arrived at his destination, little suspecting that a dozen policeman would be waiting with Thompson sub-machine guns.

And so the trap was set.

"All aboard!" called out the conductor.

The Sunset Limited, the oldest running transcontinental rail service between Los Angeles and New Orleans, was about to leave the station. The locomotive huffed and chugged, blowing out puffs of steam like the snorts of an irritated dragon. Dodge and Liz stepped up onto the Pullman car and found seats up in the observation lounge. Because it was a trans-continental train, there were no coach cars with open seating, but since Dodge and Liz were only traveling as far as Palm Springs, a mere two and half hours, there seemed little point to occupying the sleeper cars. The observation lounge on the other hand, would afford him a look at the open spaces of the American West. As he watched the buildings of downtown Los Angeles slowly disappeared behind the hills and the turns in the track, he thought about what lay ahead.

When he had announced his intention to travel to Palm Springs, Liz had insisted on accompanying him. She didn't know about the plan he and Gwinn had hatched, but since she had made it clear that, with or without his permission, she would be on the train, he had reluctantly given in. He would try to keep her safe, but he wasn't Hurricane Hurley.

He wasn't invincible, and he couldn't save everyone.

He thought about Captain Falcon and Father Hobbs, both gone now. He thought about Hurricane and Findlay Newcombe, both brave albeit in very different ways. He thought about Molly Rose Shannon and then tried to think about something else.

He tried to focus on the journey ahead. He looked at the faces in the observation car. There was a family, a father and mother with two small children. There was an elderly woman traveling with a much younger man, a grandson perhaps. There were four nuns, all with habits on their heads. There were three businessmen who appeared to be in a heated conversation. There was a lone man who had his face buried in the newspaper, and in the rear of the car were Gwinn and his men.

Then, there was Liz.

I should probably let her in on the plan, he thought, and cleared his throat to get her attention. "I have a confession to make. This trip isn't what it seems."

A mischievous gleam appeared in her eyes. "I knew it. This was all a devilish scheme to whisk me off on a romantic holiday?" She batted her eyes. "I'm flattered of course, but really, I'm not that kind of girl."

Dodge blanched. "If I gave you that impression, I sincerely apologize."

"Oh, for goodness sake. I'm teasing." She giggled, but Dodge wondered if the display of humor was a pretense to hide her disappointment that such was not in fact his intent. "Seriously though," she went on, "what is it you're trying to tell me?"

Dodge turned his gaze back to the window. "The attack at the studio…You know that I was the target."

"I kind of figured that out when they chased you all the way from the cave set to the castle."

"And since they failed, the killers will probably try again."

She nodded. "Go on."

Dodge turned back and examined her reaction. "We have decided to draw them out into the open with this little trip, to set a trap."

"'We' being you and Inspector Gwinn." She nodded toward the far end of the observation lounge where the policemen were seated.

Dodge looked surprised. "You noticed?"

"Pretty hard not to. I spent half an hour being interviewed by the erstwhile inspector. He sticks out like a sore thumb. And Palm Springs is where the Inspector and his men caught Louie Murillo, the mobster last year."

Dodge had wondered why Gwinn had been so quick to suggest Palm Springs as the place to spring the trap. Now he understood. He shook his head in amazement. "It seems you're quite the detective yourself."

"If that's what it takes to be Dodge Dalton's sidekick." She laughed. "Speaking of which, it was pretty impressive seeing you in action. Gave me all kinds of new ideas for the serial."

Dodge rolled his eyes but before he could reply, a shadow fell over him. He looked up and saw a man in a dark trench coat standing over him. His copy of the Times, which had earlier hidden his face from view, was now tucked under his arm, and Dodge could see his own name in bold type under the masthead.

The man was smiling, but it wasn't a friendly smile.

"Good evening, Herr Dalton," the man said with a distinct German accent. "I wonder if you might do me the pleasure of dining with me before we reach Palm Springs?"

Liz must have read the surprise on Dodge's face. "No offense, mister, but who the heck are you?" she asked.

"But of course, how thoughtless of me," he said removing his hat. "Allow me to introduce myself, my name is Alfred Farber. I am...what is the word? Enthusiast?"

"A fan?"

"Just so." Farber smiled. "A fan of Herr Dalton's."

Liz's gaze flashed from Farber to Dodge and back again. "Something tells me you're looking for more than just an autograph."

"This is true." Farber squinted apprehensively. "I bring news that concerns some friends of yours, Herr Dalton."

The word "friends" sent a chill down Dodge's spine. Was Farber talking about the mysterious winged killers? Or someone else?

He glanced down the length of the car to where Gwinn was sitting, wondering if he should try to alert the policeman. If the killers were making their move now, before the trap was set, they were sunk. Still, Farber hadn't done anything overtly threatening. Maybe this was an opportunity to get some answers.

"I think what Miss Sansom meant to say," he said slowly, "Is that dinner would be wonderful."

The dining car was noisy, crowded with families enjoying the fare and engaged in conversation, oblivious to the trio who settled in around a table at the rear of the car.

Dodge noticed Gwinn and his men filing in as well, and made eye contact with the Inspector, who nodded back in response. That made him feel a little better.

"Okay, Farber," Dodge said. "Start talking. Who the hell are you? I don't buy that you're a fan."

Farber allowed his lips to curl into a devious grin. "Touché. I hope you will forgive the deception. I have a passing familiarity with your writing, but it is your more recent exploits that have commanded my attention."

"Exploits," Dodge echoed. "You're German. I tangled with some Nazi spies a while back. Friends of yours?"

The smile slipped a notch. "Perhaps we've gotten off on the wrong foot. As I said, I have news that may interest you. News that concerns your friends Molly Rose Shannon and Hurricane Hurley." He slid a folded piece of paper across the table. Dodge recognized it as a telegram.

Dodge sucked in a breath. This was an unexpected turn.

"Molly?" Liz asked, incredulous. "Sorry, I sometimes forget she is a real person and not just one of your characters."

Dodge unfolded the telegram and read it silently.

INFORM DALTON WE HAVE MRS AND HH STOP BRING HIM IMMEDIATELY STOP KAUFMANN

MRS and HH. Molly Rose Shannon and Hurricane Hurley. Dodge folded the telegram again and placed it in the pocket of his suit jacket.

"Who's 'we'? Nazis? Nazis are holding my friends. Have I got that right?"

Farber's eyes narrowed. "I am a servant of the Third Reich, ja."

"Pretty gutsy move showing up here." Dodge curled his hands into fists under the table.

"I'm not alone," Farber said. He tilted his head toward a nearby table where a group of hard-looking men sat staring at them. One of them drew back his coat to reveal a holstered pistol.

"Neither am I," Dodge replied, bringing his hands into view. He was angry, but more than anything else, he knew that if he didn't act immediately, the situation was only getting worse.

"Please calm yourself, Herr Dalton. There is more going on here than your realize."

"Then why don't you start talking, buster?" Liz snapped.

Dodge felt a twinge of admiration for the plucky screenwriter. He opened his hands, placed his palms on the tabletop. "She's right. You obviously want something from me. Let's have it."

Farber smiled uneasily. "There is a situation unfolding in Egypt. My commanding officer, Obergruppenführer Kaufmann has been ordered, by Reichsfuhrer Himmler himself, to work with a man named Antonin Novotny."

"Never heard of him. Russian?"

"A Czech. He is reputedly of one the world's leading authorities on Ancient Egypt. He studied under Edouard Naville at the University of Geneva and Pierre Lacau in Paris. They say he worked with Howard Carter in the Valley of the Kings. The order to find and capture your friend, Fraulein Shannon, came from Novotny."

"Why would an Egyptologist want to kidnap Molly?"

"That is a question Ober… Herr Kaufmann has asked as well. His mission in Egypt is purely cultural in nature."

Liz let out a snort of disbelief. "Tell me another one." She gave Dodge a knowing look. "The Nazis believe in all kinds of crazy occult stuff. They're raiding archaeological sites all over the world, looking for mystical relics."

Farber looked perturbed by the interruption. "You are remarkably well informed for a…"

"For a woman? I'm a writer, pal. A damned good one, and I do my research."

"And has your research revealed who is behind the recent attempt on Herr Dalton's life?"

Dodge's heart quickened. "Something tells me it's about to."

"It is this Novotny who gave the order to capture your friend, Fraulein Shannon. And it was Novotny's men who attacked you yesterday."

Dodge drew in a sharp breath. Novotny was an Egyptologist, a digger. Had he discovered a trove of adamantine artifacts in the Valley of the Kings? A trove that included the wing devices? "You're certain of this?"

"Novotny commands a hydrogen-filled dirigible. Our agents reported that it arrived in California early yesterday morning. We do not believe his arrival on the very day you were attacked is a coincidence."

"A dirigible," Liz said. "That makes sense. Those hawkmen would have needed an elevated jumping-off point."

"What else do you know about it?" Dodge asked. "The wings they were using, do you know where Novotny got them?"

Farber shook his head. "Novotny is playing his own game, a game that Kaufmann believes may not advance the interests of the Reich, no matter what the Reichsfuhrer thinks. That is why he sent me to bring you this news.

"Novotny wants you dead. And he wants Fraulein Shannon alive and unmolested. I suspect these are not unrelated. Novotny no doubt believes you will interfere with his plan, particularly since it involves your friend. That is why Kaufmann very much wants to ensure that you do not meet an untimely end. You will be his…how do Americans say it? Wild card?"

"Ace in the hole," Liz said.

"Just so."

Dodge leaned back in his seat. It was a lot to process. Just knowing who was behind the attack was a relief, but that seemed of little import now. "You've got Molly," he said. "And your boss is going to turn her over to this Novotny?"

"He has little choice in the matter. However, you may be in a position to do something for her. My orders are to bring to Cairo, Herr Dalton."

"I can get there on my own."

"I must insist you come with me," Farber's voice took on a steely edge. "Both of you."

"Leave Liz out of this."

"I'm afraid it is you that has involved her. She will be my ace in the hole."

"I don't think you understand what that actually means," Liz said.

Farber ignored her. "No harm shall come to either of you as long as you cooperate. But if you refuse me, Herr Dalton, she will be the first to pay the price. I am sorry, but I have my orders."

Dodge leaned forward and matched Farber's piercing stare. He did not like the man. His gut told him it was all an elaborate trap engineered by the Nazis, but they had chosen the perfect bait for the trap.

"As much as the thought of helping your Führer realize his grandiose delusions disgusts me," Dodge said. "I have to help Molly. But I guess you already knew I'd say that. But Liz stays here. That's not negotiable."

Liz bristled. "I'll do my own negotiating, thank you very much. I'd like to see how this plays out."

Farber smiled and relaxed. "Excellent. I have a plane waiting in Palm Springs."

Behind Farber, the door to the dining car opened and a pair of surly looking men swept into the car. Dodge barely registered their familiar dark form-fitting body suits and the strange silvery objects attached to their backs and protruding above their shoulders. His attention was drawn to the guns in   their   hands.

CHAPTER 7– SMOKE ON THE WATER

The Royal Mail Ship Queen Mary stood 181 feet high, taller than most of the buildings that lined the dock, and weighed almost 82,000 tons. A pair of covered gangways, lined with well-trammeled red carpets and emblazoned with the logo of the Cunard White Star line, stretched from the huge vessel to the pier, which was bustling with activity. Passengers saying their good-byes, porters transferring luggage. Further down the dock, a huge crane was lifting a touring car, destined for the ship's auto deck.

The smell of fish and salt water filled Newcombe's nose as he got in the queue and gradually made his way onto the ship. He had made the trip to New York by himself. Dunn had insisted on that, which meant that the question of what had happened to Fiona remained unanswered. He had tried to occupy his mind with the other mystery, the source of the adamantine that had been used to craft the djed amulet.

He had not been completely honest with Dunn about the strange metal. While it was true that there was, as yet, no known method of processing the ore—which to the best of his knowledge had been found only in a cave in Italy—he knew with certainty that an ancient civilization had found a way to do just that. The foremost question in his mind was whether the adamantine artifact in Egypt represented yet another link to that prehistoric culture, or something entirely new. He needed to know more about the amulet, where it had been found, and whether there were more like it.

A purser took his papers and directed him to a first-class cabin. After leaving his luggage in the room, he returned to the main deck and joined the crowd gathered there to watch the departure. He scanned the throng, searching for Dunn and his companion, but saw no sign of either man.

The ship pulled away from the dock, accompanied by a fanfare of braying horns made its way out to sea. When the New York skyline was nothing more than a bump on the horizon, Newcombe returned to his cabin to wait and worry. At an average speed of thirty-one knots, the voyage would take about five days, which meant plenty of time to do both.

Shortly afterward, a purser delivered a note from Dunn, instructing Newcombe to meet him in the smoking lounge after dinner. The note, and the promise of an explanation, made the intervening span of time all the more excruciating. He picked at his dinner and then hastened to the appointment in the crowded lounge, which was filled with men of all ages smoking pipes, cigars, and cigarettes of various brands and smells. A cloud of smoke hung in the air, rising to the ceiling, and making Newcombe's eyes water as he roved through the room, looking for Dunn.

"Dr. Newcombe!" It was Sadiki. "Here. Follow me."

The man led him to a secluded corner of the lounge where Dunn sat puffing on a cherry wood pipe. "Arcadia mixture," the white-haired man announced. "One of my few remaining vices. Join me?"

"I don't smoke," Newcombe replied.

"Then you are a saner man than I," Dunn replied. He took several puffs, the tobacco in the bowl glowing bright red. "I apologize for the rather clandestine nature of this meeting, but I had to make sure that you were not being followed."

"Why would anyone be following me?"

"Why indeed? Truthfully, I do not know who to trust. His spies might be watching us right now."

"Whose spies? Professor Dunn, I must insist that you tell me what's going on."

"Yes, yes. I owe you that much." He clamped the pipe in his teeth and puffed again. "Several weeks ago, I was approached by a very influential and reputable Egyptologist who wanted my help in locating a ruin in the western desert, a lost temple to Osiris, filled with riches beside which the spoils of Tutankhamen would seem like pocket change, or so he told me. It sounded fanciful, but the given the man's reputation, I couldn't refuse. The promise of a discovery like that is what every Egyptologist lives for.

"As you know, my daughter Fiona is an archaeologist. Truth be told, a better one than I ever was, but headstrong and incautious. She helped me narrow down the search to an area in the White Desert, at the ancient boundary of the Old Kingdom. We found some artifacts, including that amulet, and had nearly pinpointed the location when my benefactor grew impatient. While he was trying to…persuade me, Fiona set out into the desert with Sadiki to find the temple."

At this, Sadiki ducked his head guiltily.

"You were with her?" Newcombe said, unintentionally making it sound like an accusation. "I don't understand why you came to me. Shouldn't you be out there looking for her?"

"I'm afraid it's not quite that simple. You see, I have learned that the man who commissioned my search…" Dunn faltered as if unsure how to proceed. "He's very dangerous, and if he finds the temple…."

"What?"

"Miss Fiona took me to the temple," Sadiki said. "Inside, we found… terrible things."

"There is a door in the temple" Dunn intoned, ominously. "A door that can only be unlocked with the djed amulet. Beyond the door…" He sighed. "Beyond it is the realm of Osiris. The Underworld of Egyptian mythology. I know, it sounds unbelievable."

"No, actually it doesn't." Newcombe felt a chill creeping up his spine. He shook his head. "I think I can guess the rest. Fiona went through this door and didn't come back."

Sadiki flinched again.

"I have studied the lore and religion of ancient Egypt all my life," Dunn went on, "But I tell you, this is something different. I fear that Novotny understands it all too well, and intends something terrible with it."

"Novotny?"

"Or a man claiming to be him. He contacted me through proxies at first, but one week ago, he came to my home in Cairo and… took me. Threatened me if I didn't find the Door of Osiris before the end of the month."

That explains the cuts on his face, Newcombe thought.

"At the time," Dunn went on, "I did not realize that Fiona had already located the temple. When Sadiki found me and told me what had happened, I feared that if I went into the desert to find Fiona, I might lead this hooded villain to the prize he seeks."

Newcombe sat bolt upright. "I'm sorry, did you just say 'hooded villain'?"

"Novotny, or whomever he is, sometimes hides his face beneath a hooded robe, like some conjurer in a street fair. I thought that, if I could understand what it is that he wants, I might be able to save Fiona while preventing him from doing whatever it is that he intends to do. That is why I came to you. Fiona has spoken of you, of your knowledge and your bravery. And, I'll confess, I had hoped that Fiona's plight might serve as an additional incentive."

Newcombe raised his hands. "Please, Professor. You don't need to convince me. Of course, I will help. But this hooded villain you speak of. If he is who I think he is, then you will need more than just me. You'll need Dodge Dalton."

"Fiona mentioned him as well." Dunn exhaled a cloud of fragrant smoke. "To be perfectly honest, I thought she was making that bit up. Isn't he the chap in those newspaper stories?"

Newcombe waved a hand. "Dodge is a friend. He'll want to know about this." He thought about the strange visions Dodge had reported in the adamantine cave in Italy, and the dreams that had been plaguing Molly Rose

Shannon. He also thought of Dodge's telephone call, about the adamantine artifact in California.

It can't be a coincidence, Newcombe thought.

"In fact," he went on, "it may explain something that he's been investigating." He rose. "I'll send a wireless message…"

His voice trailed off as he spotted a pair of men sitting by the door. They looked familiar; he was certain that they had been on the train from Boston, but what made them conspicuous was the fact that, like him neither man was smoking.

"Professor, I think you were right to be concerned about someone following us," he said slowly.

The two men were watching Dunn closely, but when they noticed Newcombe's scrutiny, they looked away quickly, and then got up and hurried from the lounge.

Newcombe jumped to his feet and started toward the exit.

"Good heavens, man," Dunn exclaimed. "Where are you going?"

"After them."

"If they are who I think they are, then those are very dangerous men."

"We're on a ship at sea. They won't dare try anything. The advantage is ours, Professor At the very least, we need to find out who they are and where they are going. Come on! Not a moment to lose."

Without waiting, Newcombe rushed through the smoke-filled lounge and burst through the doors, but the men were already gone. A moment later, Sadiki came through the doors, with Dunn shuffling along behind him, muttering. "Headstrong. No wonder Fiona fancies you."

Newcombe, who had been looking left and right for some sign of the two men, whirled around. "Fancies…?" He stopped as he caught a whiff of a distinctive and familiar odor. "Do you smell that? Smoke?"

"We are standing outside the smoking lounge," Dunn pointed out.

"No. It's wood smoke." Newcombe sniffed the air until he thought he had located the direction from which the smell was coming and then hastened in that direction.

The smell grew stronger as he raced down the corridor, in the direction of the first-class berths, and before long, he found himself wading through a pall of smoke. If he had any remaining doubts about what was happening, the ringing of bells and the echoed shouts—"Fire! Fire! Fire!"—swept them away.

Passengers began stumbling out of their cabins, many dressed in their nightclothes, fleeing before the flames. A phalanx of uniformed stewards and crewmen came rushing down the hallway, knocking on the cabin doors, ordering them to get topside, as smoke filled the corridor like a thick fog.

Newcombe pushed through both the smoke and the onrushing river of humanity. He was not a believer in coincidences. This fire, mere minutes after discovering that someone was spying on them, defied the laws of probability. The men had set the fire, and Newcombe was pretty sure he knew why.

He glanced back. "Professor, is your stateroom in this section?"

"Why, yes it is. Why?"

"I think they set the fire to cover a break-in."

"A break in. I don't…" Dunn whirled suddenly to face his associate. "Sadiki! Please tell me…"

Sadiki reached in his coat pocket and pulled out the amulet. "I have it, professor."

Dunn let out a sigh of relief. Newcombe skidded to a stop. "No sense in going that way then." He motioned for the other men toward the nearest stairwell leading down to the main deck where the rest of the passengers were already assembling. "I was wrong about these men. They aren't worried about getting caught. We are going to have to find a way to disappear, or blend in with the other passengers, otherwise I'm afraid—"

Suddenly the banister Newcombe was holding onto erupted in a spray of splinters, mere inches from his hand, followed a fraction of a second later by the report of a pistol. More shots followed, even as the three men ducked down, hiding in the smoke.

"Turn back," Newcombe shouted, staying low as he led the others back up the stairs and into the miasma. He turned away from the source of the smoke and headed back in the direction of the passenger lounges. Newcombe passed by the smoking lounge and headed for the cabin-class main dining hall.

The enormous room was empty, the dinner dishes long since cleared away, the tables with their long flowing tablecloths already set for the next day's breakfast. At the opposite end of the room was a huge map of the Atlantic that showed the route and current position of the ship, and more importantly, a door that let out onto the opposite side of the ship. Newcombe pulled the men inside and drew them down behind one of the tables.

He had studied a map of the ship during the hours spent waiting for the meeting with Dunn. Now, he tried to recall the layout of the decks. "That door leads to the sundeck. There is a wireless room not far from there."

"Wireless? Good heavens, can't that wait?" Dunn asked. "We should find somewhere to hide."

"I'm not sure we can hide from these men, professor," Newcombe said. "And we may not get another chance to send a message to Dodge."

"Your friend won't be able to help us out here."

"Perhaps not, but he needs to know who the Prisoner is."

"Prisoner?"

"The man who threatened you. Novotny."

"Why do you call him that?"

"It's a long story, and we seem to be short of time." Newcombe leaned out from behind the table and checked to make sure the coast was clear. No sign of anyone, but he decided not to risk crossing the room in the open.

Instead, he crawled between the tables, until he reached the perimeter of the room, which was decorated with stately columns and lighting sconces.

His caution saved their lives.

A few seconds after they reached the columns, two men—not the pair he'd spotted in the smoking lounge, but definitely of their ilk—darted into the room with pistols drawn.

Newcombe motioned for Dunn and Sadiki to freeze.

The gunmen moved from table to table, zigzagging back and forth flipping the tablecloths upwards in a desperate search. They worked quickly, unknowingly closing the distance with their unseen prey.

"We had better get out of here," Dunn whispered.

"Wait!" Newcombe tried to stop him but it was too late. Dunn's hip brushed against a tablecloth pulling it and everything on it, along behind him. Crystal ware and china crashed to the floor. A tumult to rival the fire alarms echoed through the empty dining hall.

Ear shattering gunshots rang out as bullets whizzed over their heads. Shards of glass rained down on them, as the crystal drinking glasses on the tables above them exploded. Each bullet that connected pelted the floor unmercifully with the tiny projectiles.

Newcombe and the others crawled away as fast as they could, each movement causing the tiny particles of glass to imbed in their hands. Sadiki cried out, but kept moving. They reached the end of one table, the next was just a few yards away, but it might as well have been a thousand miles, for at that instant, one of the gunmen appeared directly in front of them, his smoking pistol pointed right at Dunn.

CHAPTER 8— IN THE WIND

"We need to get out of here," Dodge said, sliding out of his sea and reaching for Liz.

"Novotny," Farber said with a scowl. "I was too late."

Dodge caught Inspector Gwinn's eye and nodded in the direction of the approaching threat. Farber meanwhile turned to his henchman seated across the aisle, and shouted. *"Holt sie euch!"*

In an instant, the dining car was transformed into the O.K. Corral. Guns appeared as if from nowhere, and the air was filled with the noise of battle and the screams of frightened diners seeking cover beneath their tables. Bullets riddled the walls of the car, shattering windows and splintering wood. The smell of gunpowder and woodsmoke stung Dodge's nose as he pushed Liz down, and maneuvered her toward the nearest exit.

He did not wait to see who was winning the battle, but pushed through the door and out onto the gangway that connected the dining car to the next coach. He didn't know where they would find safety, but moving away from the gunmen seemed like the most expedient course of action.

The rush of air through the vestibule surprised him. The gangplank crossings between Pullman cars were enclosed with an accordion-like articulated coverings to keep passengers safe and comfortable when moving up and down the length of the train, but for some reason, the roof of the vestibule had been peeled back exposing them to the rushing wind of the train's passage. As Dodge stared up through the opening, wondering about this, a hand reached through and seized hold of his arm, plucking him effortlessly off his feet.

For a fleeting second, Dodge was airborne, flying in the wind of the train's relentless advance through the California desert. He felt weightless, like a kite borne aloft, and then just as abruptly, he slammed down on top of the coach. The wind—the same air current that had so gently lifted him up, now tore at him with what seemed like the force of a hurricane.

He slid and tumbled a few feet, before arresting himself by grabbing hold of a streamlined air vent cowling. It was all he could do to hold himself there while he gasped for breath. The air was full of coal smoke and grit, blasting him at sixty miles per hour—the speed of the train as it bolted through the open desert. Through the blinding spray Dodge saw a figure moving toward him.

It was a hawkman, his wings tilted in such a way that the wind pushed him down, holding him fast atop the train's roof, enabling him to withstand the violent rush of air.

"We were just talking about you," Dodge shouted over the roar of the wind. The words came out in short little gasps. "Why don't you fly back and tell Novotny to come down here and do his own dirty work."

As if taking Dodge's advice, the hawkman tilted his wings, spreading them wide and was caught away in an instant. He spiraled up, gaining hundreds of feet of altitude in the space of just a few seconds, then appeared to simply fall....

No, it wasn't a fall. It was a dive.

The hawkman arrowed toward Dodge, like an eagle swooping down to pluck a rabbit from the prairie. Dodge knew if he let go of the air vent that the wind would scrape him off the roof of the train car, but if he stayed where he was, the hawkman's razor sharp wings would slice him to ribbons.

He searched his memory of the battle with the winged killer on the Republic backlot, trying to remember what had worked then, but every strategy he could think of would require at least one more hand than he had.

Gonna have to risk it, he thought. He drew himself up to a kneeling position and hooked a leg around the vent cover. The hawkman was coming in fast, but the train was moving at a fair clip too, protracting the dive and giving Dodge a few extra seconds to whip his belt off, slip the buckle through the vent opening, and cinch the leather around his ankle with a hasty knot.

He looked up just as the speeding hawkman spread his wings wide, leveling out mere inches above the top of the train, just a hundred feet behind Dodge.

Dodge let go of the vent and stripped his suit jacket off. The wind whipped at the garment and holding onto it would have been a Herculean task, but holding onto it was not Dodge's plan.

He held the coat over his head and let go.

The wind snatched the jacket from his fingers, briefly eclipsing his view of the flying killer and, with luck, the killer's view of him.

The flying jacket abruptly reversed direction as it wrapped around the hawkman's head and began moving up the length of the train, straight toward Dodge. The hawkman, unable to see but moving too fast to do anything but stay the course, lowered his wings so the tips were scraping along the top of the roof, plowing twin furrows that would have eviscerated anything or anyone in their path. Dodge however had taken advantage of the killer's momentary blindness to remove himself from the danger zone. Instead of pressing himself flat in a futile attempt to avoid the deadly bladed feathers, Dodge launched himself out of his crouch, above the wings, and right at the hawkman's covered head.

The impact was like a blow from a wrecking ball. Dodge heard a crunch of breaking bones and, judging by the spike of pain that shot through his body, they might have been his own. Stunned, he bounced away and landed flat on his back beside the vent and started sliding toward the edge of the roof, but then he felt something tighten around his ankle—his belt, still hooked to the vent cowling.

The hawkman bounced back too, stopped dead in mid-flight, like a bug splattered on the windshield of car. As he slid away, the wind seized Dodge's jacket again and in the instant before his body toppled from the roof of the train car, Dodge saw the hawkman's head lolling limply from a broken neck.

Dodge heaved a sigh of relief and lay there for a few seconds before pulling himself back to the vent, and then cautiously, with arms and legs spread-eagled to prevent himself from sliding away to oblivion, began inching back toward the end of the car. When he reached it, he lowered himself down through the tear in the vestibule cover and dropped onto the gangway beside a stunned Liz.

"Your pants are falling down," was all she could say.

Suddenly Farber burst through the door, accompanied by the sound of more gunshots. "Go!" he shouted. He aimed his pistol through the door and squeezed off two shots, then hustled them across the gangplank and into the next car which appeared to be the baggage car. He slammed the door shut behind him and urged them to keep going. "My men are dead," he panted. "So are your policemen, I fear. We scored a few hits, but those wings of theirs stopped our bullets."

Dodge felt a pang at the thought of Gwinn and his men, dead at the hands of Novotny's henchman, not to mention the dozens of innocents who might have been injured in the crossfire

"I think one of them might be wounded," Farber continued, "but…"

"But they won't stop until I'm dead," Dodge finished.

"Novotny is a madman."

"We need to get off this train," Liz said.

"Jumping from a train at this speed will kill us just as surely as those hawkmen," Dodge said. "Right now, we just need to stay alive."

He looked desperately around the compartment. There was no shortage of places to hide, but all of them looked too obvious. There trunks and suitcases piled along the wall, Stacked in front of them were bags stamped with stenciled letters that read United States Postal Service, each one big enough to….

"Quick, give me your shoes."

"What?" Farber and Liz asked in unison.

"Trust me."

A roar like a cyclone filled the baggage compartment for a moment, but the sound died just as quickly when the last remaining member of Novotny's assassination squad closed the door behind him. Over the rhythmic rumble and clank of steel wheels on the tracks, the sound of his footsteps was faintly audible. One injured leg was dragging, creating a two-part harmony. Step. Slide. Step. Slide.

The steps and slides moved closer to where the three survivors of the massacre hid and then that noise stopped as well. The assassin leaned over one of the mailbags, studying something that protruded slightly from the opening at the end, and then, after a few agonizing moments, spoke.

"Clever." The man's accent, along with his olive complexion and dark hair suggested a Mediterranean or possibly Arab ethnicity. "But not clever enough. You have wrapped yourself for delivery to my lord Osiris. He awaits you in Hell."

The man aimed his pistol and fired. The noise of the report cracked in the close quarters of the baggage car, and the air was filled with the smell of sulfur. The man fired a second shot, then changed his aim and fired again.

The slide assembly on his automatic pistol locked back, exposing a long section of the barrel. The magazine was empty; the last bullet fired. The man withdrew a spare magazine from a pouch on his belt and started to reload.

"Now," Dodge shouted, and gave a hard push to the towering stack of suitcases behind which he, Liz and Farber were hiding. They pushed too, and the entire stack folded over to crash down on the assassin.

The impact dislodged the weapon from the man's grasp, but to Dodge's astonishment, the man leapt out of the way of the luggage avalanche, and with a speed and grace that belied his injuries, pounced on Dodge like a striking leopard.

The punches landed like lightning strikes. Dodge threw his hands up to cover his face, but the man simply aimed his blows lower, pummeling Dodge's chest. Desperate, Dodge threw his hands out and caught hold of one of the mail bags—the very same one into which he had slipped his shoes in order to create a decoy—and heaved it at his attacker. The blow knocked the man off him, but before Dodge could regain his feet, the man recovered. His eyes darted away from Dodge, just for a second, and then he dove to the floor.

His gun!

The pistol came up. The slide shifted forward with a click, racking the round into position, and the barrel moved ever so slightly until its business end was point right at Dodge. "Goodbye, Mr. Dalton."

Without the shielding effect of the luggage barrier, the noise of the report was almost deafening. Another shot followed immediately, but the first one had done the trick.

The man's head snapped back as the rounds from Farber's pistol punched through his skull.

Dodge sagged in relief, barely noticing when Liz crawled out from behind the pile of bags to give him a hug.

"Do you feel that?" Farber said. "The train is slowing."

"I'm not surprised," Dodge replied. "I don't think there's been a shootout on a train since the days of the Wild West."

"This is our chance," the German said. "We must go now."

"Go where?" Liz snapped.

"He's right," Dodge said. "Novotny is still out there. He has more men and he's not afraid to send them after us. If we're still on this train when it stops, we'll be sitting ducks. And a lot of innocent people might get hurt in the crossfire."

"If we can get to telephone," Farber said, "I can arrange for a car to take us the rest of the way to Palm Springs where the plane is waiting."

"What about Inspector Gwinn?" Liz asked. "And everyone else?"

"The best thing we can do for them is to go somewhere far, far away. Somewhere like Egypt."

CHAPTER 9— CAPTAIN'S PREROGATIVE

"You are needed in Egypt, Herr Professor," the gunman snarled. "We are here to take you back."

Newcombe's heart stuttered in his chest. He had read the situation completely wrong. These men weren't assassins and they weren't burglars here to steal the djed amulet. They were kidnappers.

The second gunman stepped into view behind them, his gun lowered as well. There was nowhere to go.

"How do you propose to take us anywhere?" Dunn shot back, trying to hide the nervous quaver in his voice. "We're in the middle of the ocean."

The man's lips twitched into a smile. "We have made arrangements," he said cryptically. "Sadly, your friends won't be continuing along with you."

The muzzle of his weapon shifted a few degrees until it was pointing at Newcombe's heart.

"Wait, I—"

Newcombe jumped at the sound of the shot. Strangely, he felt no pain.

Several more reports followed in close succession and then the gunman toppled backward like a felled tree. As the smoke cleared, Newcombe saw both men sprawled on the deck.

A commanding voice rumbled through the dining hall. "You can come out now, gentlemen."

Newcombe lifted his head cautiously and spotted a pair of men in the black uniforms of ship's officers, both holding revolvers at the ready. One of them—Newcombe realized with a start that it was the ship's captain himself—holstered his pistol and turned to the other. "Take them to my quarters. And assign a detail to collect those bodies. This place needs to be ship shape before breakfast. I don't want the passengers inconvenienced any more than they already have been."

The junior officer put his gun away and stepped toward the three figures still cowering behind the table. "Gentleman. If you would please follow me."

The abruptness of the rescue made it feel more like an arrest, but as they followed the officer through the maze of corridors and companionways, Newcombe decided the brig—did the cruise liner have a brig?—was probably the safest place for them.

Instead of a cell belowdecks, the officer escorted them to stateroom overlooking the bow. The room was lavishly appointed, with bird's-eye maple and cherry wood paneling on the walls. There were several chairs and couches arranged around small tables, a built in bookcase that housed volumes of leather bound publications, a small oak desk with a separate filing hutch, and a small wash basin with soap and towel. Blue velvet curtains matched the fine cloth carpet, making the room seem more like a cocktail lounge for VIP guests than a jail cell.

"Have a seat, gentleman," the officer said. "The captain will be with you shortly."

He was not mistaken. No sooner had the three men settled in when the captain stormed through the door. "I hope one of you has a good explanation for what's been happening tonight."

Newcombe exchange a glance with Dunn, wondering how much to tell the captain, though in truth, he really didn't know the answer to that question.

When no one spoke, the captain settled in behind his desk and crossed his arms over his chest. "Well, let's start with your names."

Newcombe seized on the opportunity. "I am Dr. Findlay Newcombe, currently a professor of applied physics at MIT in Boston and scientific advisor to the President of the United States of America. Perhaps you've heard of me?"

It was evident from the complete lack of recognition in the captain's stony gaze that he had not.

Somewhat chastened, Newcombe went on, gesturing to his visibly shaken companions. "This is Professor Padraig Dunn from the University of Egypt, and this is his manservant, Sadiki."

The captain narrowed his eyes at Dunn, then he abruptly stood and walked over to his bookcase. His eyes roved over the spines for a moment until he found the title he sought, removed it, and returned to the desk, where he dropped the book, face up. The volume landed with a slap that seemed almost as loud as a gunshot in the ominous quiet. "Would you be the same Professor Dunn who wrote that?"

Newcombe shifted forward to read the lettering on the cover. *Uncovering the Secrets of the Egyptian Gods.*

Dunn's eyes lit up, his fear ebbing away. "My goodness. I thought only universities carried that book."

"Where do you suppose I found it?" the captain returned, gruffly. "I studied archaeology at Oxford. That was before I discover my true passion of course, but I occasionally indulge my curiosity about ancient civilizations. Call it a hobby."

Dunn enthusiasm faltered at the implicit putdown of his life's work, but he had found his voice. "Captain, I shall speak plainly. I'm afraid all this ruckus might have something to do with an artifact that we are carrying. Sadiki, would you show him?"

Sadiki took the talisman from his jacket pocket and placed it on the desktop for the captain's inspection. The officer's eyes flitted toward it briefly, but he made no move to touch it.

"A djed amulet," he mused. "Hardly seems worth the trouble of sabotage and attempted murder."

"Nevertheless, I believe this is what they were after." Dunn sagged back in his chair. "The amulet…and myself."

"You?"

"The amulet may be the key to finding a lost Egyptian temple. We are on our way to Egypt to conduct that search. Obviously, these men must have wanted me to take them to it."

The captain smiled, but it was a look of satisfaction without any trace of humor. "I knew there had to be more to it than mere petty theft. But why attempt to abduct you here, aboard ship? We're in the middle of the Atlantic. Why not wait until we made port? If, as you say, you were already bound for Egypt, why not wait until you got there?"

Dunn spread his hands helplessly. "Perhaps they didn't realize where we were going."

"And what were they going to do with you once they had you?"

Newcombe cleared his throat. "Captain, while we may not have all the answers, I can assure you that protecting Professor Dunn and keeping this discovery out of the wrong hands, is a matter of great importance to the U.S. government."

"In case you hadn't noticed, Dr. Newcombe, this is His Majesty's ship."

"All the same, I'd like to send word to a friend of mine. Dodge Dalton. Perhaps you've heard of him?"

"Can't say I have." The captain gave a dismissive wave then snatched up the book, passing it back and forth between his hands. "My only concern is the safety and well-being of the passengers. That includes you of course, but if there are more of these hooligans about, your presence here puts the rest of us at risk. That fire could have been catastrophic."

"I assure you, sir, we are—"

The captain raised a hand, cutting Newcombe off. "I think it would be best for all concerned if you left my ship."

"Surely you don't intend to cast us overboard."

The captain chuckled. "It's tempting, but I have a better idea. If, as you say, this affair involves the security of the United States, then I suspect His Majesty's government may have an interest in speeding you on your way.

"And how do you propose to do that?" Newcombe asked. "As you say, we're in the middle of the Atlantic Ocean."

"Archaeology wasn't the only thing I learned at Oxford." He returned the book to the shelf and then strode toward the door. "Come along."

The decks were still crowded with frightened passengers wearing life-vest over their evening clothes, nervously waiting for one of two commands: All clear, or abandon ship. Newcombe could hear their fearful whispers of pirates and foreign saboteurs. The fire had long since been extinguished, but did that mean the danger had passed?

The all clear bell rang just as they reached the wireless room just off the Sun Deck, but it was evident from the discontented murmur that the passengers needed further reassurance. As they passed by, Newcombe could not help but wonder if the crowd concealed more villains intent on abducting Dunn and killing the rest of them. He studied the faces, looking for that hard edge that he had seen in the eyes of the two killers from the dining hall.

"You may be right about putting us off being the only way to insure the safety of your passengers," Newcombe told the captain, "but how in heaven's name are you going to get rid of us?"

"An old mate of mine from Oxford is with the Admiralty," the captain said. "Some of us rose higher than others. If this affair is as important as you claim, I'm sure he can be persuaded to send one of His Majesty's naval vessels our way."

"And if not?"

"I'm sure we can spare a lifeboat."

Dunn's eyes went wide. Newcombe patted his shoulder. "He's joking, of course. You are joking, sir, are you not?"

The captain did not reply but entered the wireless room, a cramped windowless box lined with wires and gauges. Four desks, each manned by a radio operator, were positioned against the walls. The captain approached one of them and spoke in a low voice. "In need to place a telephone call to the Admiralty."

"Telephone?" Newcombe said. "Is that even possible?"

"The Queen Mary has full telephone connectivity to anywhere in the world," one of the other radio men said in a voice filled with pride.

"Remarkable," Newcombe said. "The future is already here, gentleman."

The captain shushed him and then spoke into telephone handset. He succinctly explained the situation to man on the other end, then listened for a long time, only occasionally interjecting a comment. Finally, he handed the receiver back to the crewman, signaling the end of the call.

"We're in luck, gentleman," he told them, gesturing to the door. They passed out onto the Sun Deck. "The *HMS Hunter* is close by. We'll rendezvous with her and she will bear you the rest of the way

"To Southampton?"

"To Egypt. Port Said. It seems you were not exaggerating about the importance of your mission. The Admiralty seems as eager to have you in their care as I am to be rid of you."

As they returned to the now mostly deserted deck, Newcombe could not help but notice a man lurking near the rail, his back turned to them, casually smoking a cigarette. Unlike most of the passengers, even the steerage class, who saw the trans-Atlantic voyage as a chance to dress their best, this man was wearing dungarees and a pea coat. He glanced their way for a fleeting instant, just long enough for Newcombe to get an uneasy feeling.

He quickened his step and leaned close to the captain. "Sir, I may be horribly mistaken, but I think that fellow over there might be another one of the villains."

The man must have had eyes in the back of his head, because he immediately flipped his cigarette out into the sea, and started in the opposite direction.

The captain reversed step and gave chase at a brisk but determined walk. "Sir, may I have a word with you."

The man froze in his tracks, staring straight ahead, one hand slowly reaching into the pocket of his coat.

The captain whipped his pistol from its holster. "Do not make any sudden moves, sir. I have a weapon."

The man slowly withdrew the hand, which was curled into a fist, and then raised both of his hands in an apparent sign of surrender. Then, he abruptly brought his right hand to his mouth.

Stop!" the captain shouted, thumbing back the hammer of his pistol. The man jerked his hand away as if in compliance, but a moment later, he slumped to the deck as if he had fainted. The captain rushed toward him, as did Newcombe and the others, but it was already too late. The man's body had gone rigid and white froth was oozing from his clenched teeth.

Newcombe caught a whiff of a familiar chemical smell, like burnt almonds. "Cyanide," he muttered.

The captain was aghast. "What the devil? He killed himself rather than be caught? Utter madness." He kneeled over the man and began to search the pockets of the heavy jacket. He found a semi-automatic pistol, but nothing that might have identified the man.

"It seems we have another unidentified corpse on our hands," the captain said. He raised his head to one of the officers. "Put him with the others, but be discreet about it." He then turned to Newcombe and shook his head. "Nazi spies, I'll wager."

"How do you know?"

"I told you the Hunter was close. What I didn't tell you is that they have been shadowing a German U-boat. And that U-boat has been shadowing us."

Newcombe swallowed nervously, then looked at Dunn. "Nazis," he repeated. "You didn't tell me there would be Nazis."

"It's dry," Hurricane remarked to Wittgenstein. "But other'n that, it's about as inviting as those sewer pipes back at your college."

"At least we could breathe in those," Molly said.

She wasn't wrong about that. Despite the chill—the metal bulkheads seemed to suck the warmth right out their bodies—the air was thick, the smell almost overpowering. Hurricane felt winded just sitting still.

That was all they had been doing for hours now. Sitting still in a cramped compartment aboard the U-48, under the watchful eye of an armed Kriegsmarine sailor.

"Shhhh!" Their minder waved his pistol, a Luger P08 semi-automatic.

Hurricane chuckled. "If you're so worried about the noise, why don't you just go right ahead and pull the trigger there, Fritzy?"

The German submariner muttered something in his native language and waved the gun again in a threatening matter.

"Why are they so worried about the noise?" Molly asked. She spoke in a barely audible whisper to avoid incurring any reprisals from the guard, even though, as Hurricane had just pointed out, there was no way the Germans would risk shooting them. If they had wanted to do that, they would have done it hours ago when plucking them out of the North Sea.

"There are two way to hunt submarines," he explained, keeping his own voice low to avoid causing any further distress to his companions. "You can spot 'em from the air, though that's tricky especially at night. Or you can listen with a hydrophone. Noise travels for miles underwater, and with sonar, you can figure out pretty quick where a submarine is if they're making even a little bit of noise. You can bet the Royal Navy is listening. Comin' into British waters was a pretty gutsy move."

"Where are they taking us?"

"Perhaps I can answer that." This new voice, speaking heavily accented English, was loud enough to make even Hurricane jump a little. A man wearing civilian clothes and a heavy coat came up behind the young guard and dismissed him. "No need to whisper," he went on. "We are safely away from England and soon we will be able to surface and continue on our way."

"Surface?" Molly said. "I thought the whole point of an undersea boat was that it's supposed to go below the surface."

"Travelin' underwater is a real drag," Hurricane said. "Literally. These boats can go twice as fast on the surface." He looked back at the newcomer. "You said something about answers, Fritz?"

The man's face screwed up in a distasteful frown. "I did. And the name is Jungen Müller."

Hurricane waved his hand as if shooing away an irksome fly. "You ain't in uniform. I'm guessing you're SS. An honest to goodness Nazi."

"A very astute observation, Herr Hurley." Müller put his hands on his hips, and as he did, his coat opened just enough to reveal a very familiar looking pistol in a very familiar looking shoulder holster rig.

"Now that's a mighty big gun you've got there," Hurricane said, nodding at Müller. "I used to have one or two just like it. Be careful with it. You might not be man enough for that much gun."

Müller grinned defiantly.

"I'll be getting them back," Hurricane continued. "Depend on it."

"What's this about, Mr. Müller?" Wittgenstein asked in a more diplomatic tone. "Why did you capture us at gunpoint? Surely you must realize how dangerous such an action is. You could provoke a war."

Müller regarded the philosopher with an amused expression. "Herr Professor. Finding you with these two was an unexpected pleasure. The Fuhrer will be delighted to hear of your capture."

The German, perhaps noting Molly's questioning look, went on. "Didn't you know? Our Fuhrer attended the same school in Linz. Herr Wittgenstein made quite an impression."

Judging by the contemptuous tone, Hurricane could only assume that impression had been a bad one.

"Funny," Wittgenstein replied. "He made no impression on me whatsoever. Not then at least. Now my impression is that he's a barbarian. No. That's too kind. Barbarians are at least human beings."

Hurricane hid a smile.

Müller regarded the professor with cold indifference. "As I said, the Fuhrer will be delighted to hear that we have you."

"Wait a sec," Molly said. "You said it was unexpected… This is about us? Me and Hurricane?"

"No, Fraulein Shannon. It is about you. Only you."

Molly shrank back, pressing herself into Hurricane's chest. "What do you want with her?" he said.

"Alas, even if I were inclined to tell you, the truth of the matter is that I don't know. I was ordered to deliver Fraulein Shannon to my superior in Egypt. Alive and unharmed. It seemed prudent to bring you and Herr Professor Wittgenstein along, if only to ensure her cooperation." He turned his gaze back to her. "If you remain compliant, no harm will come to your companions. Not while I have anything to say about it, that is."

"Egypt?" Hurricane said. "Why Egypt? What's there?"

Müller shrugged. "Pyramids. Camels. Arabs. And the answers you seek. I'm afraid that's all I know."

He straightened as if preparing to depart. "We have a long journey ahead of us, but there is no reason for it to be unpleasant. But if you are entertaining thoughts of escape, allow me to remind you that there is nowhere to go. And there would be consequences."

Without waiting for an acknowledgement, the German spun on his heel and left. The young sailor with the gun returned, but this time, he maintained a respectful distance.

"Egypt," Wittgenstein said. "Why the devil do you suppose we're headed there?"

"I'm truly sorry that I got you involved in this, professor," Molly said.

He leaned over and gave her a hug.

"I reckon we're going to need a miracle to get out of this," Hurricane said. "Fortunately, we've got a few days to dream one up."

The professor straightened abruptly. "Good heavens. Where is my mind?"

"You got something for us, Wigsteiner?"

Wittgenstein turned to Molly, an urgent look on his face. "The answers aren't in Egypt, my dear. They're in you. Or more precisely, in your dreams about your father. That's why you came to see me, after all. We need to speak with him?"

"And how on earth are we supposed to do that?"

"Through hypnosis, obviously," Wittgenstein said. He reached down into his pocket and pulled out one of the few things the Germans had allowed him to keep, his pocket watch.

"Freud thinks dreams are nothing more than the manifestation of our sexual anxieties," Wittgenstein continued. "It's hogwash of course. If you unravel a dream, and take the content of it to be accurate and without symbolism, then you can dig deep into the heart of the matter. There is no symbolism, no Greek mythology employed here. Freud is wrong, and I have told him so on several occasions rather emphatically."

"So, you're going to hypnotize Molly and do…what, exactly?" Hurricane asked somewhat confused.

"I told you," Wittgenstein said holding the watch. "We're going to ask her father to explain why he's visiting her in dreams."

Hurricane nodded slowly in comprehension. He shot a glance at the young sailor assigned to guard them, wondering if the man would interfere.

Probably not. The Nazis were likely just as interested in what was going on in Molly's head as they were.

"The mind is an intricate mechanism, much like this timepiece." He held the watch up for her to view, and then with a deft turn of his wrist set it moving back and forth like a pendulum. "It only takes the right craftsman to open it up to access the pins and levers that make it tick. When it comes to the human mind, I am that master craftsman. I am that bridge between your dreams and reality."

"I don't believe in hypnotism," Molly said, but her tone sounded more fearful than skeptical.

Hurricane reached out to her, but Wittgenstein waved him off without breaking eye contact with Molly. "That's fine dear. The important factor in this equation is that I do. For this to work, I am the only one that truly matters."

Hurricane watched Molly closely to see if would indeed work. Wittgenstein continued speaking in a calm, soothing voice, talking about the watch and the mysteries of the human mind, timing his words to the hum of the submarine. Molly stared back, almost defiantly at first, but then her eyelids began to droop, and a moment later, she was...

Standing in a forest clearing. The smell of the jungle—hot, fetid, as alive as it is deadly—is thick in her nostrils, but there is another scent too.

Meat, roasting over a fire.

She remembers this moment, this place, or something very much like it. She had been only an infant at the time, but she knows beyond the shadow of a doubt where she is…and when. Her parents camped here as they made their way up the Congo River, bringing the word of God to the natives forced to work the rubber plantations.

She turns slowly and sees the fire. A pair of spitted game birds are suspended above the flame, but there is no sign of—

Mother?

—the person tending them. Just beyond the fire, a tent has been erected, but Molly knows that if she goes to it, throws back the flap and looks inside, she will find it empty.

The memory is empty.

She turns away, heading into the trees and spies the mission, Father Nathan Hobbs's church on the river bank. Her memories of this place are much clearer, yet in those memories, there are always people. Father Hobbs's flock. Her dad's flock.

Unlike the camp, more a product of her imagination than an actual memory, this place is very real to her. She doesn't remember the parents of her blood, but only the father of her heart. Father Hobbs.

Dad.

She looks for him, looks for anyone, but the mission is deserted, and before she can approach the chapel, it bursts into flames.

In a moment the flames are everywhere, the memory peeling away in sheets of flame and ash like the pages of a book slowly being consumed in a furnace.

This memory is also empty. The mission is gone. Her dad is gone.

As the world turns to cinders around her, it's as if the curtain separating one reality from the next has been drawn back. The sky burns red. The air is scorching hot, reeking of brimstone. The ground is black, the color of charcoal, but everywhere she looks, there are white stones the size of skulls….

They are not stones.

"Molly girl?"

"Dad!" She starts to turn in the direction of the familiar voice, but he speaks again, quickly.

"Don't. Don't look at me."

She freezes despite herself.

She knows what he has become. The gatekeeper between the Dominions. The one who will unleash destruction upon the world. His body, as far she knows, is still trapped deep underground in a hidden chamber underneath the Udayagiri caves of India, but his consciousness…his soul…has been transformed into something terrible. In order to hold back the demons that will inevitably one day bring destruction to the world of humankind, he has become like them.

Only a monster can fight a monster.

"I'm not afraid to look," she says.

"I know," he replies. "I'm the one who's afraid."

"Why are you coming to me in my dreams? Who…what is the Prisoner?"

"You already know the answer."

"Captain Falcon," she says. "Or that thing that took over his mind. But Captain Falcon defeated him."

"The Prisoner's spirit was dispossessed, but he endured, wandering the world until he could find a new host. An empty vessel, waiting to be filled."

Molly shakes her head. "I don't understand."

"The Prisoner is but an echo of what he once was. He cannot simply take another person's body by force unless that person's spirit is already destroyed by despair. He found such an empty vessel in the deserts of Africa."

"Egypt?" It is a question but she already knows the answer. "The Prisoner is working with the Nazis."

"They do his bidding, imagining that they will gain control of the power to rule the world. But the Prisoner seeks only to destroy it."

"What can we do to stop him?"

"You cannot stop him."

She senses that there is more he wants to say, but instead of elaborating, he changes the subject. "Tell Dodge—"

"Dodge isn't here," she snaps, and then immediately regrets it. "He…I…After India, I left him. I couldn't…" She shakes her head. "He's in California."

"No. He's already on his way to Egypt. Find him. Tell him to take you far, far away, where the Prisoner can never find you."

"Why? We beat him once before. We can do it again."

"When we stood against him before, he sought only to rule the world. Now he desires to ruin it, and that is a far easier thing to accomplish. He believes he can regain control of the entities he once imprisoned in pillars of adamantine—the very entities that I am holding back—so that he might once again wield their power as a weapon. He does not realize that he has become their instrument, their puppet. When he has freed them from my control, nothing will prevent them from laying waste to the world."

"What does he want with me?" she asks.

"There are other gates—places where the membrane separating realities is weakest. Even now, he searches for the Osiris Gate in the deserts of Egypt."

"Osiris...What's that got to do with me?"

"He will find it. That is why you must flee. You must hide. But know this. One day he will find you and when he does, he will use you to destroy me. The link between us is the bridge that he will cross. It is a link that only death can break."

"What are you saying?" She whirls around to confront him...and stops.

He is not a monster, not the demon of the abyss. Not the Child of Skulls. He is just her dad. And he is weeping as if his heart is broken beyond repair.

"Oh, Molly girl. I told you not to look."

She realizes that his warning was not for her sake, but for his. She is her dad's last remaining link to the world of mankind. Both an anchor and a lifeline. If anything happens to her....

Now she understands why the Prisoner wants her. She is the weapon he will use to break her father's hold over the otherworldly entities, and unleash destruction upon the world.

"I'll find Dodge," she promises, blinking away the tears. "Dodge will stop him."

She takes a step toward him, opening her arms, but he retreats. "No. I can't bear it. Go. I have lingered here too long already. It's time for you to...

"Wake up," Wittgenstein said, snapping his fingers.

Molly's eyelids fluttered open. A hint of brimstone lingered in her nostrils a moment longer, but as her focus returned, the smell of the U-boat—diesel oil and body odor—gradually supplanted the memory.

"I . . ." She faltered, gazing first at Wittgenstein, then at Hurricane. "Did it work?"

"I was about to ask you," Hurricane said, his voice a concerned rumble.

"You achieved a trance state," Wittgenstein said. "But I was unable to communicate with you. It was most unusual. Do you remember anything?"

"Yes. I saw . . ." Even as she tried to grasp hold of the memory, it slipped away like the last dream before waking. She shook her head. "It's gone now."

"Crazy idea anyway," Hurricane grunted. "Guess it's back to the drawing board, eh, Wigsteiner?"

"At least we know what the Prisoner wants now," Molly said.

Hurricane and Wittgenstein both snapped their heads toward her. "And what is that, Miss?"

"The Osiris Gate." She wrinkled her forehead in confusion as the unfamiliar words passed her lips. "I don't know where that came from."

"Osiris is an Egyptian god," Wittgenstein said, a thoughtful gleam in his eye. "The god of the underworld, the realm of the dead. Interesting. And you have no idea where you heard that name?"

For a fleeting instant, Molly thought she might just be able to draw up the memory, but the harder she tried, the further away it slipped.

"Well, it's a place to start," the professor said, managing a wan smile. "And we are on our way to Egypt."

So is Dodge, she thought, but before she could wonder at this, it too slipped away.

"You lot must have friends in high places," Commandant James "Sonny" Auld said as Newcombe and his companions were escorted into his office. He was an imposing figure, six feet tall with a barreled chest that seemed barely contained by his naval uniform. He rose to his feet and regarded the three of them suspiciously. "It's not every day that the Royal Navy tasks one of her destroyers to play passenger ferry for a civilian. A Yank and an Irishman at that."

Newcombe noted that Auld had omitted mention of Sadiki. "It wasn't our friend, Commandant, but a friend of the captain of the Queen Mary. I believe he and your superior were once classmates."

"There you go," Auld grunted. He sank into the chair behind his desk and fidgeted with the bamboo bowl of a tobacco pipe protruding from his pocket. "Of course, sometimes those old acquaintances cut both ways. I knew both of them at Oxford. Where did that get me? They took my ship and sent me to this hellhole."

"I would think his would be highly sought after post," Dunn said. "The Suez Canal is the single most strategically important waterway in the world."

"That's why it's such a lion's den. Nazis and Fascists skulking about, the French…who knows what side they're on. Mark my words, war is coming."

"To Egypt?"

"To the whole world. God, what I wouldn't give to have a ship under me again." Auld sighed and leaned back in his chair. "Anyway, you're here now. Welcome to Port Said, gateway to the Suez. I've been ordered to continue accommodating your needs, whatever they may be." He eyed them cautiously. "What, ah, might they be?"

"I don't know how much you've been told—"

"Precious little," Auld complained.

"We're on our way to Farafra Oasis," Newcombe continued. "Unfortunately, Nazi agents are dogging our heels."

Auld sat up a little straighter. "Nazis?"

"They sabotaged the Queen Mary in an attempt to abduct Professor Dunn, here."

Auld cast a skeptical eye at Dunn. "And what makes you so bloody important?"

Dunn bristled at the coarse language. "Now see here—"

Newcombe hastily intervened. "The Nazis think Professor Dunn can lead them to lost treasure. He's one of the world's leading Egyptologists."

"Is that a fact? My predecessor left those behind. Are they worth anything?" Auld jerked a thumb over one shoulder, gesturing at a row of figurines on a dusty shelf behind the Commandant's desk. Even to Newcombe's untrained eye, the statuettes appeared, stylistically at least, to be of ancient Egyptian origin. He sucked in a breath when he saw that one of the figures was almost identical to the djed amulet Sadiki carried.

Dunn appeared to notice the similarity as well. He rose and circled around to the display picking up the lookalike artifact. He turned it over in his hands. "A cheap forgery for the tourists," he declared. "My apologies, Commandant. But on the bright side, you'll have no difficulty clearing customs with it if you want to send a souvenir back home."

Auld gave a dismissive wave. "As if I'd want anything to remind me of this benighted place. May as well bin the lot."

Dunn shrugged and retook his seat.

"In any case," Auld went on. "You've convinced me of your bona fides. I can't spare the men to take you to Farafra. I can get you as far as Cairo, but I'm afraid that will be the limit of His Majesty's assistance."

Despite his seeming indifference to their plight, Auld evidently took the threat to their safety seriously, providing not only a car and driver, but an escort of Royal Marines—one man with a rifle joined them in the sedan, while two others riding motorcycles bracketed them on the road—one leading, one bringing up the rear.

As exhilarating as the motorcycle ride must have been, Newcombe did not envy the two men as they rolled down the scorching hot, dusty road. The going was slow, the rough road crowded with animals and humans alike. The marine riding ahead of them kept tooting his horn, and gesturing angrily for the herds and beasts of burden to clear out of their way, but it was a Sisyphean task.

"This could take a while," Dunn remarked. Almost as soon as he said it, the road abruptly cleared, like the sea parting in some Biblical miracle. Their driver, seizing on the opportunity, punched the accelerator.

Suddenly, the motorcycle ahead of them fell over, spilling its rider onto the road.

"What the devil—?"

Their driver reacted instantly, slamming on the brakes and cranking the steering wheel hard. The rear of the car slid around, throwing up a screen of dust even as stones began pelting the engine hood.

No, Newcombe realized. *Not stones. Bullets.*

"The Nazis!" he gasped. "They've found us."

Just as the driver got the sedan turned around, a bullet from the unseen sniper caught the motorcyclist who had been bringing up their rear. He flew over his handlebars and crashed in a heap almost directly in front of them.

The marine sitting beside them leaned out the window, searching for a target with his Lee-Enfield rifle, then slumped over the frame, a ragged hole between his shoulder blades.

Three men dead, and Newcombe hadn't even heard a single report. "Get us out of here," he shouted.

The driver needed no encouragement. He stomped on the accelerator and charged back down the road leading to Port Said, but a hail of bullets continued to rain down on them. The car's back windshield shattered, sprinkling the three passengers with shards of glass. The driver weaved back and forth, trying to make it as difficult as possible, but no matter which way he turned, the fusillade quickly followed.

"Where the devil are they?" the driver rasped. He swung the sedan off the main road and headed down a narrow alley, swerving to avoid a pack of dogs. Low hanging clotheslines slapped at the bullet-ridden vehicle, but for the moment at least, the attack seemed to abate.

"I've got to get us back to the Port Commandant," he said. "They won't dare attack us on British territory."

There was a loud thump on the roof of the vehicle. Not a bullet, but something much bigger. Newcombe looked up and saw the metal bulging inward, as if something heavy had been dropped onto the car.

Something or someone.

The metal sprang back into shape as the weight was removed, and then Newcombe spied movement through the front windshield. The driver slammed on the brakes and the barely glimpsed figure stepping down onto the hood of the car was hurled forward, but instead of tumbling down the alley the attacker swooped up into the sky like a....

"Hawkman!" Newcombe gasped, recalling the word Dodge had used.

The flying attacker pirouetted in mid-air and then swept right back to where he had been, alighting on the hood of the sedan. One silvery wing flashed in the late afternoon sun, and the windshield shattered inward.

The driver jerked as if stung and then his head tipped over and fell from his shoulders.

With an ear-splitting shriek, the roof of the sedan peeled back like the lid on a sardine can, exposing the three passengers to the sky. Above them, half a dozen more hawkmen circled like vultures, and higher still, a silvery airship floated in the sky like a second moon.

"Oh, God," Dunn whispered. "He's here."

The airship shuddered as its pilot fought to keep it on course. The gondola creaked under a near constant assault from the hot desert wind. Newcombe felt a little nauseated, no doubt a combination of the unrelenting motion and the horror of the attack on their convoy, which had culminated in their being brought aboard the dirigible. He now sat next to Dunn and Sadiki in a corner of the gondola, under the watchful eyes of two hawkmen. Their wings were folded behind their backs, giving them a perversely angelic appearance.

A door opened and a middle-aged man with white hair and shockingly colorless eyes stepped into the compartment. He wore a tweed jacket with a white handkerchief square protruding from the breast pocket. Compared to the hawkmen, he seemed rather ordinary, like a faculty professor, but Newcombe sensed that this man was far more dangerous than the winged killers. This suspicion was confirmed when Dunn grabbed Sadiki's arm, fear draining the blood from his face.

"The Prisoner," Newcombe murmured.

The man knelt before Dunn, fixing him with a dead-eyed stare. "Professor. I believe my instructions to you were clear. Imagine my surprise when I found out that, instead of searching the desert for the Door of Osiris, you had lit out for America."

"I'm here, aren't I?" Dunn replied in a tremulous whisper

"Indeed you are. How curious." The Prisoner's lifeless eyes flicked toward Newcombe, just for instant, then returned to Dunn.

"I needed help. This man…" He gestured to Newcombe. "Is an expert on the metal—"

"I don't care," the Prisoner said, cutting him off. "All that concerns me is whether you have located the Door."

"The Door is useless to you without the key," Dunn said.

The Prisoner stiffened, his eyes coming alive with anger. "How do you know this?" He gripped Dunn's shoulders and shook him. "You've been there, haven't you? It's the only way you could know. You've known where it is this whole time."

"Yes," Dunn wailed. "I didn't tell you because I… I didn't…"

"Fool." The Prisoner thrust Dunn away from him, slamming him against the bulkhead, but then he seized hold of him again. "You will take me to Door. Tonight."

"Yes, yes," Dunn said. His tone was pleading, but Newcombe saw a defiant gleam in the old man's eyes. "I'll tell you where to go. Just don't hurt Fiona."

"If you are deceiving me, you won't live long enough to see what I'll do to your daughter, professor." Newcombe thought he might make good on the threat right then and there, but after a moment, the Prisoner seemed to master his rage. "Forgive me, my dear professor. You cannot imagine how long I have dreamed of this day, when I shall fulfill my destiny and enter the Osiris Gate. Alas, I shall have to wait a little longer. There is something I need at Farafra Oasis."

CHAPTER 12– TWILIGHT AT THE OASIS

Through the side window of the Junkers *Ju-90* transport plane as it made its approach to the Almaza Aerodrome northeast of Cairo, Dodge could see forever. Not that there was a lot to see. The landscape below was a mostly featureless expanse of sand, framing a vast verdant triangle; the Nile Delta, where the longest river in the world discharged into the Mediterranean Sea, bearing hundreds of miles worth of nutrient rich sediment. He strained his eyes for a glimpse of the famed pyramids of Giza, but if they were there at all, they blended so perfectly into the golden landscape that he could not distinguish them.

The lumbering aircraft descended and touched down with a shudder on the macadam, and made its way to the hangars comprising the aerodrome. The field was a hive of activity, with planes of varying sizes showing the flags of several countries from around the globe. German Focke Wulf *FW 200 Condors* were lined up next to British deHavilland *Albatrosses*. There was even a lone Douglas *DC 3* from the United States. Although it seemed to be business as usual on the ground, Dodge knew that the presence of these aircraft was symbolic, or perhaps symptomatic, of a deadly political game being played out not only here, but around the world. Throughout its history, Egypt had been the focus of attention for great empires. Until only recently, Egypt had been, in varying degrees, under British control, but since the signing of the Anglo-Egyptian Treaty of 1936, the British military presence had been restricted to the Canal Zone, leaving a vacuum in which foreign agents vied for control of the nation's strategic location and resources to support a looming conflict that would be played out on the world stage. The current power struggle between England and Nazi Germany was just the latest iteration of a timeless cycle.

As the plane came to a stop and the four BMW 132 Radial engines driving the main props cut out, Dodge unbuckled his seatbelt and joined Liz and Farber at the exit. The air rushing in through the open hatch was sharp and hot, like the blast of heat from an open furnace door.

"It's like we never left Palm Springs," Liz remarked, fanning herself with a hand.

"If you've seen one desert," Dodge remarked. "You've seen one too many."

Although there had been a few tense hours following their leap from the Sunset Limited, the journey across the world had been mostly uneventful, punctuated by a few refueling stops where they had been given the opportunity to stretch their legs and not much else. Farber had kept them on a short leash, and offered little in the way of enlightenment as to the purpose behind the Nazis' interest in Dodge, fending off inquiries with the assurance that his superior would explain everything once they arrived in Egypt. But as Farber stood at the top of the stairs leading down from the aircraft, gazing at the empty tarmac, Dodge got the impression those answers would not be immediately forthcoming.

"I don't understand," Farber murmured. "Where are they?"

"Looks like you got stood up," Liz said.

"Obergruppenführer Kaufmann knew that we were arriving. I had assumed he would want to meet you personally."

Dodge spied a brown smear across the horizon in the distance. "I hope our ride shows up before that dust storm gets here."

"Maybe we can hitch a ride with those guys," Liz said pointing at two vehicles—a long-bodied Mercedes Benz 770 grand touring car, and a shorter, utilitarian MB-G5—were racing down the tarmac toward them. The tops of both vehicles were down, revealing men in dusty brown military uniforms conspicuously carrying compact machine pistols. Their caps were adorned with a distinctive eagle and swastika badge, and their collars bore the paired lightning bolt insignia of the Nazi SS, but none of the men appeared to be as old as Farber. Dodge guessed they were low ranking enlisted soldiers.

"Not who you were expecting, Färber?" Dodge asked

The German frowned but motioned for them to follow. As he approached, the driver of the lead vehicle got out and threw up his hand in the customary salute. Farber waved dismissively and fired off a question in German. Farber relayed the answer to Dodge and Liz.

"Obergruppenführer Kaufmann awaits us at Farafra Oasis," he explained, sounding none too pleased. "Four hundred and fifty kilometers from here."

Liz gasped. "Four hundred and fifty? How far is that in real miles?"

"A little over two hundred," Dodge said. He turned to Farber. "You're kidding right?"

"I'm afraid not, Herr Dalton. Get in. Make yourselves comfortable. We have a long day ahead of ourselves."

"I'm beginning to wish I'd stayed in Palm Springs," Dodge muttered.

It was nearly dusk when they arrived at the remote oasis, but long before they reached the inhabited settlement of Farafra, Dodge could tell they were descending from the desert plateau, into a cooler, wetter geographical depression. It was still desert, but a considerably milder desert than the one they had traveled through to get there. The settlement itself, though sparsely populated, had the feel of a resort getaway—not unlike Palm Springs—but Dodge was acutely aware of the fact that he and Liz were essentially Farber's prisoners, isolated and completely reliant upon the Nazi.

If it was a trap, they were already caught.

The cars drove though the center of the settlement, the dirt road lined with simple block buildings plastered with desert mud, and continued a ways beyond to a walled compound that looked like it might have been a thousand year-old ruin. As they pulled through the arched gateway—there was no actual gate—into a courtyard with a bubbling fountain, Dodge spotted the soldiers with machine-pistols standing watch on the battlements.

As the cars pulled to a stop, a figure emerged from the main structure opposite the fountain and strode briskly toward them. He wore a leather jacket and a peaked military cap with the now all-too-familiar badge of the German Nazi regime's paramilitary arm, the Schutzstaffel. For no reason that Dodge could fathom, he had a long riding crop tucked under his left arm.

Farber leaped from his seat and snapped off smart salute. "Herr Obergruppenführer. May I present Dodge Dalton."

"You must be Kaufmann," Dodge said, not waiting for Farber to complete the introduction. "We've waited long enough for some answers. Now you've brought us out here to the middle of nowhere."

Hurricane probably could have expressed more colorfully. He missed his big friend, and not just because he knew how to turn a phrase.

"I just want to know two things," he continued. "Where are my friends? And just what the hell is going on here?"

Kaufmann sniffed the air as if he found Dodge's presence, to say nothing of his question, distasteful. "Your friends were picked up off the coast of Britain two days ago by one of our Unterseeboots. Even at top speed, it will take the U-48 at least four more days to reach Egypt. Be assured, they are safe for the moment." He narrowed his gaze. "As to your second question, I assume Farber told you about Novotny. He wants you dead, Herr Dalton."

"Right. I kind of figured that out when his goons tried to chop me up for fish bait. Farber told me who, but he didn't tell me why. Why does he want me dead? I've never even heard of the guy."

"He fears you," Kaufmann said. "That is something I find most interesting. Why does a man who can bend the Third Reich itself to his whim, fear a writer of childish stories? When you know what a man fears, you have power over him."

Dodge ignored the jab. "He's afraid of me. You're afraid of him. That doesn't answer my question. Why? And why are we out here?"

Kaufmann returned an icy smile, then looked past Dodge, gazing through the gateway out into the desert.

"You expecting someone?" Liz asked.

"As it happens, I am. But please, come inside. We can discuss this over some refreshments." Without waiting for a reply, he spun on his heel and headed toward the main building. Farber gestured for Dodge and Liz to follow.

Dodge looked at Liz and shrugged. "Might as well."

They followed Kaufmann into the building which, on the inside at least, resembled a colonial manor house, albeit one badly in need of remodeling. Dodge guessed the Germans had only recently occupied the house, and probably had no intention of remaining there one day longer than absolutely necessary. Nevertheless, the interior was warm and welcoming, and the smell of baked bread and something savory filled the air. Kaufmann led them to a dining room with a long wooden table and invited them to sit while Arab servants decanted water from crystal carafes into matching goblets.

Liz took a greedy sip but Dodge kept statue still and focused on Kaufmann. Although Farber had not exactly been a font of information, during the course of their long journey, Dodge had developed a working hypothesis about Novotny. The only remaining question for him was whether the

Nazis were willing partners or reluctant pawns. Clearly, Kaufmann resented Novotny's influence, but that didn't automatically make him Dodge's ally.

"So what are we doing out here in the middle of..." He waved his hand, once more wishing Hurricane were there to supply some colorful adjectives. "Egypt?"

Kaufmann's look of irritation deepened, but he laid his hands palm down on the table top in front of him. His fingers curled around the ends of the riding crop. "The Third Reich has a cultural interest in Egyptian history. The Egyptians were the first truly great civilization on Earth, erecting monuments that have stood fast against the march of time. They possessed technology that even modern man cannot fully comprehend, secrets that are only now coming to light. I believe they were true Aryans."

Liz nodded meaningfully in the direction of the Arab servants. "Maybe they'll share if you say 'pretty please.'"

Kaufmann's lips flattened in a tight smile. "The Egyptians who built the pyramids are no more. Their line was mongrelized, weakened. They were conquered by Greeks and Romans, and eventually supplanted entirely by these Arab barbarians. No, the secrets of the ancient Egyptians lie beneath our feet, buried in the sands of time."

"Very poetic," Dodge said, disingenuously. "Sounds like something I might write in one of my childish stories. What exactly is it you think you're going to find?"

"Have you ever heard of the Dendera Lights?"

Dodge gave an imperceptible shake of his head.

"In the Dendera Temple complex at Hathor, there is a relief that depicts a djed pillar with human arms holding up a snake within the lotus flower. Some of our preeminent scholars recognized this arrangement as an electrical lighting system. The djed pillar is a power pylon, and the snake is symbolic of an electrical current." Kaufmann's smile deepened. "You Americans cling to the myth of Benjamin Franklin discovering electricity. Hieroglyphic inscriptions, dating back as far as 2750 BC, have been discovered that describe Egyptian priests harnessing the power of electrified fish and using rods of amber to attract lightning. The Egyptians mastered electricity thousands of years ago using the technology of the Aryan master race."

"Are you kidding?" Liz asked, incredulous. "You're trying to find an ancient Egyptian light bulb? I guess you fellas haven't heard about another American, Thomas Edison."

"She's right, Kaufmann," Dodge put in. "You don't seriously expect us to believe that's all this is?"

"The Dendera Light is only the beginning. An outward manifestation of a power that we cannot comprehend. A power that Germany alone will possess. You see, Herr Dalton, it is so much more important than a mere light bulb."

Kaufmann was not lying, but Dodge sensed he wasn't telling the whole truth. Regardless, the man's ambitions were all too familiar. *Find an ancient source of unlimited power and rule the world,* he thought. *Where have I heard that before?*

"And Novotny? What does he want?"

Kaufmann gripped the riding crop, flexing it as if doing so helped him control a building ire. "Ostensibly, he shares the goals of the Reich. He is a well-respected Egyptologist. An expert in his field."

"But?"

"But Farafra Oasis is hundreds of kilometers from the Dendera Complex. It makes no sense. Nor does his demand that we bring your friend, Fraulein Shannon, to him here. He is playing a game and I do not know what it is."

"Maybe I can help you with that," Dodge said.

"You?" Farber intoned. "You did not even know who Novotny was?"

"No, but I know who he really is. Those wings his goons use to fly around like circus performers? They're made of an extremely rare metal called 'adamantine.' No one alive today possesses the knowledge to work with that metal, to say nothing of actually creating devices like those wings. Those things were made thousands of years ago by an ancient civilization."

Kaufmann lowered the crop to the table and looked at Dodge with a hungry expression. "Go on."

"That civilization disappeared long ago, but some of their stuff turns up every now and then. I found some in Antarctica a while back. My guess is that Novotny found some as well. Those wings, and probably a lot more he hasn't told you about."

Like the Prisoner, Dodge thought, but didn't say.

It all made sense now. The Prisoner—the entity who had once possessed Captain Zane Falcon—had found a new puppet in the form of the Egyptologist Novotny. It was the only possibly explanation. How else would he have come to possess adamantine artifacts and know about Dodge and Molly?

"More?" Kaufmann said thoughtfully. "Like what?"

"Like the power to destroy the world. That's what he's after."

"Interesting."

"Interesting?" Liz gasped. "Try 'terrifying.' If what Dodge says is true, it's like giving matches and gasoline to a child."

"The scientists of the Third Reich are not children, Fraulein Sansom. And what you have told me is consistent with what we already know."

So he was holding back, Dodge thought.

"Tell me," Kaufmann went on. "Have you ever heard of the Black Sun?"

Before Dodge could answer, Liz spoke out. "I have. It's a Nazi fairy tale. You believe the world is hollow and that there's a tiny little sun at the center of the earth." She glanced over at Dodge and said in a low voice. "I read all about it when I was working on the Black Legion serial."

"There are some fanciful aspects to the tale," Kaufmann admitted. "But the Black Sun is real. It is a conduit to the energy of the cosmos—unlimited energy. The ancient race you spoke of possessed this power. We will also."

"It nearly destroyed them and everything else," Dodge said. "But it's Novotny you should be worried about. He's not going to just hand it over to you, you know."

"I do know. That is why I did not simply allow him to kill you." He glanced past Dodge for a moment then rose to his feet. "And now, I must say good night."

"We haven't even eaten dinner," Liz complained.

"As it happens, I am expecting another guest for dinner. I will arrange for something to be brought to your room."

"Novotny," Dodge said. "He's coming here."

"He should be arriving shortly. I'm sure you'll agree that it is in everyone's best interests that he remain unaware of your presence here." He turned to Farber. "Take them upstairs."

As if on cue, a line of uniformed SS troopers gripping machine pistols filed into the room, none too subtly reminding Dodge that he and Liz were not guests.

Definitely not guests, Dodge thought, staring through the iron bars covering the window of the upper story room where Farber had left them. He turned to Liz. "Sorry I dragged you into this."

"I seem to recall that I refused to stay behind," Liz said.

"I should have tried harder." He gripped the bars in his hands and tried shaking them loose. They didn't budge. "So how would the 'real' Dodge Dalton get out of this mess?"

Liz looked around, searching for inspiration. The room was evidently being used for storage of excess furniture. Chairs and couches, covered in sheets, lined the walls. Tables were stacked high with baskets and vases, all covered in a thick layer of dust.

"One of us could pretend to be sick," she suggested. "Then when the guards come to check on us, we knock 'em out. Take their uniforms and guns and sneak out."

Dodge raised a skeptical eyebrow. "Seriously? That's your plan?"

She frowned and put her hands on her hips. "What's wrong with it?"

"Maybe stuff like that works in the movies, but I doubt these guys are that gullible. And even if they believed us, they're killers. Do you think they'll care if we have upset tummies?"

"Well what's your great idea?"

"Still working on it." He turned back to the window. The room was situated on the west side of the main house, looking out into the desert beyond. "Even if we make it out of this room, we'll still be…"

He trailed off as he glimpsed a line of headlights moving down the road toward the compound. "Company's coming."

"Is it Novotny?"

"Not sure yet." The lights were eclipsed by the corner of the house, but he pressed his face against the bars and was able to see a slice of the courtyard as the convoy pulled in through the gate.

From his vantage, all he could make out was a single car, a G5, driven by a soldier in a brown SS uniform. A second trooper stood behind him, manning a machine gun mounted on a swivel. Neither man got out, but something was clearly happening behind them. Dodge heard men shouting orders shouted in German and then something else, a booming stentorian voice.

"Didn't your momma teach you manners, Fritz? Help the lady down."

Dodge's heart skipped a beat. Unbidden, a shout ripped from his chest. "Hurricane! Is that you?"

He listened. There was a commotion and more shouts—too many voices to differentiate, but he was certain of what he had heard. It was Hurricane Hurley. And if Hurricane was here, then the "lady" could only be Molly.

"Hurricane! Molly!"

Behind him, the door burst open. He turned just as an SS trooper charged into the room, brandishing his weapon, shouting a harsh command in German that needed no translation.

Dodge raised his hands in surrender, but before he could do much else, Liz snatched a vase off a nearby table and slammed it into the back of the Nazi's head.

The trooper dropped like the proverbial sack of potatoes.

Liz let the broken pieces of the vase fall and met Dodge's stare, her fierce expression giving way to a grin of triumph. "Hah!"

"Not bad," Dodge admitted as he knelt to relieve the unconscious trooper of his weapon. "Stay behind me. This could get dicey."

"Dicey" was an understatement. He had no idea how they were going to make it past Kaufmann's men, but the wheels were already in motion. At least there was a sliver of hope. Hurricane Hurley was there, along with Molly. If he could reach them, they might have a fighting chance.

The shout still echoed in Molly's head. She tried to listen, even as the troopers, at Müller's urging, manhandled her, Wittgentstein and, with somewhat more difficulty, the struggling Hurricane Hurley, out of the truck and toward the large house, but the shout did not repeat. Had she imagined it?

No. It was real. Someone had shouted her name.

Dodge.

Tell Dodge....

In that instant, it all came back to her. The memory that had eluded her for days, as they traveled, first by U-boat, then airplane, then automobile across the desert, returned in an instant.

Her father, standing on the doorstep of Hell itself, warning her about what was coming.

He's already on his way to Egypt. Find him. Tell him to take you far, far away, where the Prisoner can never find you.

Dodge is here. In that house.

"Hurricane," she called out. "Save your strength."

"You should heed the Fraulein's advice, Herr Hurley." A man wearing a leather jacket with SS insignia stepped out from the house and leveled a pistol at Hurricane. "I need her alive. You however are inconsequential."

Hurricane stopped resisting but did not appear the least bit intimidated. "You and me have different ideas about the definition of 'inconsequential.'"

"Easy Hurricane," Molly muttered, and then lowered her voice to a whisper. "Dodge is here."

He winked at her and she realized that he already knew it.

And then, like a wish come true, Dodge was there, standing on the porch, right behind the Nazi, holding the muzzle of a machine pistol to the side of the man's head. "Kaufmann! Tell your men to back off."

The Nazi—Kaufmann—stiffened, but then his cold smile returned. "You surprise me, Herr Dalton. I had not expected such rash behavior."

"Sorry," Dodge shot back. "I'm improvising."

"Surely you don't think you can escape."

"It's working so far. Now, tell your men to back off."

Kaufmann nodded tersely and Molly felt the hands holding her fall away, but the troopers continued watching their commanding officer, waiting for a signal to act. Hurricane pulled away from his captors and took Molly's hand, pulling her out of their reach.

"Wigsteiner," he said, his familiar confident rumble now fully restored after days of captivity. "Get over here."

Wittgenstein jolted as if waking up from a dream, and hastened forward,

"Good to see you," Dodge said, looking over Kaufmann's shoulder.

Molly wasn't sure whether he was addressing her or Hurricane, and before she could ask, an attractive woman with light brown hair and a pert nose stepped from the house right behind Dodge.

"Likewise," Hurricane said, filling the awkward silence. "I reckon we've got some catching up to do."

"It can wait," Dodge said. "Right now, we're all going to get in that truck and get the hell out of here."

"What's to stop them from coming after us?" the woman with Dodge asked.

"Two things," Dodge said. "We'll disable those cars before we go. Shoot the tires out. And Kaufmann here is coming with us."

"I like the sound of that," Hurricane said, deftly plucking a machine pistol from the hands of the nearest Nazi soldier.

Kaufmann laughed, softly at first, then louder until the sound was echoing off the walls of the compound. Except it wasn't an echo Molly was hearing, but a low droning hum, like the sound of an engine, and it as coming from the sky.

"You're too late, Dalton," the laughing Nazi said. "Novotny is here."

Half a dozen hawkmen swooped down from the night sky to roost atop the wall surrounding the courtyard. They were armed with rifles, all of them aimed in Dodge's direction.

He ducked behind Kaufmann, but the Nazi just laughed again. "Do you think they care if I live or die?"

"I'll chance it," Dodge said.

"He's right, Dalton." Farber said, stepping out from the midst of the troopers. "They have the advantage. They won't hesitate to kill all of us."

Farber was a Nazi and nobody Dodge wanted for a friend, but Dodge knew the man was right. He lowered the gun and took a step back from Kaufmann, even as Novotny's dirigible came into view above them.

More of the winged men began descending, trailing long mooring lines attached to Novotny's dirigible, and landed in the courtyard. They looped the ropes around anything stationary—palm trees, the fountain, even the parked vehicles—and began hauling the airship down out of the sky.

Hurricane, Molly and the man with them—Dodge knew it had to be Ludvig Wittgenstein, the philosopher his friends had crossed the Atlantic to consult with—walked slowly to the porch to stand with Dodge, but everyone else remained stock still as the airship was reeled in like a prize catch.

As the bottom of the gondola bumped against the ground, a door opened and a rather ordinary looking man with white hair stepped out, followed by even more hawkmen.

"Herr Novotny," Kaufmann called out. "Welcome to Farafra Oasis. Your arrival could not have come at a more opportune moment."

Novotny turned his head slowly, appraising the scene into which he had just intruded, but then his gaze locked onto the group standing on the porch of the main house. He extended an accusatory finger at Dodge.

"What is he doing here?"

For the first time since the appearance of the airship, Kaufmann looked unsettled. "Dalton is our prisoner," he said. "My men accomplished what yours could not."

"I didn't want a prisoner. I wanted him dead. Don't think I don't know what you're trying to do, Kaufmann." Before the Nazi could make any further excuses, Novotny looked away from Dodge. "Which one of them is Shannon?"

"Me."

Dodge's heart dropped like a stone. It wasn't Molly but Liz who had stepped forward, head held high. "I'm Molly Rose Shannon."

His heart dropped even lower when Molly herself spoke up. "I don't know who the hell you are lady, but you aren't me."

"Nice try sister," Liz said, defiantly. "But I'm the genuine article."

Novotny's gaze flickered between them for a moment, then he turned away. "Take them both," he told his men. "And get rid of the excess baggage."

Two of the hawkmen strode forward, while two more hastened inside the gondola ahead of their master.

Hurricane stepped out to block their approach to the two women, but Dodge placed a hand on his arm. "Don't," he cautioned. "They'll cut you to ribbons."

Hurricane shot him an angry look, which made Dodge feel even more helpless, and shook free, but the two hawkmen, sensing his intent, unfurled their wings threateningly.

"You're no good to them dead," Dodge insisted.

This second admonition appeared to be no more persuasive than the first, but just then, two figures tumbled through the open door of the gondola and went reeling across the courtyard. Hurricane's expression went from outraged to confused. "Newton?"

Dodge looked and saw that one of the two men who had just been ejected from the airship's cabin was indeed his friend Findlay Newcombe.

What's he doing here?

There was no time to pose the question. Dodge grabbed hold of Hurricane and tried to drag him out of the way of the menacing hawkmen. "We'll get them back, but we need to be smart about this."

With a harsh oath, the big man relented, stepping back and allowing the hawkmen to seize hold of Molly and Liz. Both women kept their heads high as they were marched to the gondola.

"Novotny!" Kaufmann called. "I've kept my part of the bargain…"

Novotny, ignoring the Nazi, climbed into the gondola.

"Novotny! You promised us the Black Sun!"

One by one, the hawkmen followed their master. Those who had perched on the wall swooped down to the courtyard and filed into the airship's cabin as well, leaving only the men stationed at the mooring lines. Right on cue, the latter untied the ropes and held onto them as the dirigible lifted off.

Dodge rushed to Newcombe's side and helped him up. The scientist's expression was a mixture of surprise and dismay. "Dodge! Hurricane! I…" He looked around helplessly. "Well this is a pickle."

"That's okay, doc. With your brains and Hurricane's brawn, we'll figure a way out of it."

"Novotny!" Kaufmann shouted again, then broke off his protest with a harsh curse. He turned to Farber. "Assemble the men. We'll track them."

Farber jerked a thumb at Dodge and his friends. "What about them?"

Kaufmann stared at Dodge for a moment, as if trying to decide how much trouble he was worth. "Herr Dalton, it seems Novotny is not as intimidated by you as I thought. Can you give me one good reason why I should not simply execute you?"

"I can," Newcombe said quickly.

Kaufmann frowned. "And who are you?"

"Dr. Findlay Newcombe. Professor of..." He shook his head. "That's not important. What is important is that I know where Novotny is going." He glanced over at the man who had been thrown from the gondola and was still cowering on the ground. "Or I should say, Sadiki here does."

"Very well," Kaufmann said, nodding slowly. He turned to Farber. "Spare the native. Kill the others."

Newcombe stared back in dismay. "Well that was unexpected."

"Not really," Hurricane muttered.

"Ja wohl." Farber turned to Dodge, apologetic look on his face. "I'm sorry Herr Dalton. This was not my intention, but orders are orders."

"You just keep tellin' yourself that," Hurricane rumbled. "Maybe the good lord will believe you, come judgment day."

Farber's face twitched into a contemptuous smile. He barked an order in German and two of the SS troopers stepped in close to drag Sadiki away. The rest leveled their weapons in preparation to carry out the rest of Kaufmann's command. As soon as Sadiki was clear, Farber raised his hand.

Something wooshed through the air behind the German. At that same instant, a shout of alarm went up, followed almost immediately by the thunder of multiple gun shots. The weapons were no longer aimed at the prisoners however. The Nazis were shooting into the sky.

"Hawkmen!" Newcombe shouted, his cry barely audible over the tumult of gunfire.

In an instant, the courtyard devolved into total pandemonium. The execution squad scattered, running in all directions, seeking cover from the airborne attackers who swooped back and forth above them, all but invisible against the deepening darkness.

Farber continued to look down at Dodge, his hand still raised, but there was something different about him. Dodge was still trying to figure out what it was when Farber's arm, along with everything above his sternum, slid sideways and dropped with wet plop on the paving stones of the courtyard.

The German had been sliced in half.

"Down!" Dodge threw himself flat and felt the rush of air as a hawkman's deadly wing passed through the space he had been occupying only a moment before.

"Dodge," Hurricane shouted. "We're sittin' ducks out here. We need to get inside."

Inside sounded like a very good idea. He scanned the courtyard for the missing member of their group and spotted Sadiki crawling under one of the parked military vehicles. "Go!" he shouted without looking back. "I'll catch up."

As he watched Dodge scurry off across the courtyard, like a brave sheepdog chasing down a stray lamb, Hurricane felt a pang of regret for his anger at Dodge's earlier intercession. Dodge was no coward and he loved Molly every bit as much... *No,* he corrected himself, *He loves her more than life itself, even if he can't figure out how to tell her that.*

Dodge had probably saved Hurricane's life, and living to fight another day sure did beat the Hell out of the alternative.

Right now, living to fight another day definitely involved getting under-cover where these circus freaks with razor sharp wings couldn't reach them. He grabbed Newcombe by the scruff of the neck with one hand, caught hold of Wittgenstein with the other, and made a dash for the porch of the house.

A Nazi trooper spotted the movement and tried to block them, but before he could level his smoking machine pistol, a swooping hawkman flashed through the air between them.

"Much obliged," Hurricane muttered as he nimbly hopped over the disassembled remains of the Nazi and kept going, barging through the front door. Unfortunately, the battle had already reached the interior of the house.

Kaufmann, the Nazi commander was locked in hand-to-hand combat with a grounded, but by no means defenseless hawkman. Several dead Nazis were strewn about the room, but they had managed to take a couple of the hawkmen down with them. Hurricane surmised that the attackers had entered the house through an upper story window, or possibly cut an opening in the roof, and then made their way down, cleaning house as they went.

The hawkman seized Kaufmann by the throat and lifted him into the air, then slammed his body down onto a table which collapsed upon impact, throwing up a choking cloud of dust. Kaufmann curled into a fetal ball. The hawkman turned his body, raising one wing in preparation to deliver the coup de grace, but as he did he caught sight of Hurricane standing in the doorway with the others. The killer's face was mostly hidden by his get up, but Hurricane would have sworn he saw the fellow smile.

"Go!" He shouted, thrusting Newcombe and Wittgenstein toward the stairs. He didn't know if the second story of the house was clear or an ambush waiting to happen, but to stay where they were was certain death. The hawkman ignored the two scientists and advanced toward Hurricane, slashing the air with his wings.

"We'll see how tough you are after I pluck your feathers, pigeon-man," Hurricane said as he slowly side-stepped toward the nearest fallen Nazi. The dead man's gun lay beside him on the floor, wisps of smoke still curling from the barrel.

As Hurricane started toward it, the hawkman, anticipating the move, slashed down with his wings, cleaving the gun in two and cutting a deep gash in the floor. Hurricane however had twisted away at the last instant, the move toward the gun a feint. His real goal was the Nazi corpse, or more precisely, a familiar object affixed to the dead trooper's belt. In a single fluid motion, he scooped up the corpse and heaved it at the hawkman, and as he let go, he pulled the igniter strip of the Model 24 *Stielhandgranate*—stick hand grenade.

The hawkman, still recovering from his failed attack, was half-a-second too slow. Before he could swat the flung corpse away, it slammed into him and bowled him over backwards. Hurricane used the moment to leap behind an overturned desk. The stick grenade had a five second fuse, and as he counted down to zero, he covered his head and braced himself for the detonation.

...Two...One...Zero...Boom!

Except, there was no boom.

The only sound was the muffled noise of the battle outside.

The grenade was a dud.

The problem with dud grenades was that sometimes they weren't duds after all. They might hang fire for a while and then go off as soon as you poked your head up for a look-see. Once the igniter was pulled and the five seconds were done, it was a crap shoot.

Lady luck strikes again.

The hawkman was almost certainly back on his feet and that meant at any moment his razor sharp wings would hack through the desk.

Can't stay here, can't move, he thought, and then it occurred to him that he could actually do both.

He lowered his shoulder to the flat desktop and started pushing, scooting the heavy desk across the floor like the blade of a bulldozer. There was a thump as the sliding desk hit something but he kept pushing, picking up speed. Another thump and something silver flashed through the air above his head.

Got him, he thought, and kept going, driving the desk, along with the stunned hawkman and everything else that happened to be in his path—which included one very unpredictable live hand grenade—all the way across the room until he hit the wall with a sickening crunch.

He scrambled back, staying low while putting as much space between himself and the capricious explosive device as the room would allow. He glanced at Kaufmann, still dazed and writhing amid the shattered remains of the table and then in the corner of his eye he glimpsed another familiar face, or rather, a familiar head.

"Hello there, Herr Müller," Hurricane muttered. "You have something of mine."

He looked around until he spotted the rest of Jungen Müller. Both of his wrists were bent at an unnatural angle from his outstretched arms, and to either side of him lay Hurricane's custom-made .50 caliber semi-automatic pistols.

Müller had gotten a couple shots off before meeting his maker, but it had cost him dearly.

"I warned you," Hurricane said. He stripped the holster rig off the headless corpse and slung it over one shoulder. Müller had modified the straps to accommodate his smaller frame and there wasn't time to readjust it, but just having the pistols in his hands again was almost enough to make him believe his luck was finally changing.

Naturally, that was when the grenade finally detonated.

Less than fifty feet separated him from the open top vehicle where Sadiki had taken refuge, but it was fifty feet of sheer hell. The air in the courtyard had become a choking miasma of gunsmoke. Directly above Sadiki, a trooper was manning the mounted machine gun, spraying lead into the sky.

The car rocked with each burst. The stones of the courtyard floor were littered with hot brass shell casings that rolled painfully under Dodge's hands and knees as he crawled toward his destination. Thankfully, the hawkmen were too busy meting out destruction upon the Nazis, and the Nazis were too preoccupied with defending against the surprise attack, to notice one defenseless figure crawling for cover.

After an eternity that probably lasted no more than ten seconds, he reached the cowering Sadiki and crawled under the car next to him. "We can't stay here," he shouted.

Another machine gun burst shook the vehicle, but then abruptly ceased. There was a strangled cry and the trooper's body dropped to the ground beside the car.

Sadiki's stared at the dead soldier like a shell-shocked doughboy contemplating another push across No-Man's-Land, but then nodded. "I know."

"I'm going to start this car up. As soon as you hear the engine turn over, you need to climb in. Got it?"

"We won't be safe in the car," the other man said. "Their wings can cut through anything."

"Our only chance is to get away from here while they're busy fighting the Nazis. Sooner or later, whoever wins this battle will come after us."

Sadiki nodded again. "Yes. I understand."

Dodge took a deep breath. "All right. Here goes nothing." He scrambled out on the far side of the car and opened the door. The interior of the vehicle was littered with shell casings from the now abandoned machine gun. Dodge swept the hot brass out of the way and crawled into the driver's seat, keeping his head down.

The engine turned over on the first try. "Sadiki. Come on!"

For a few seconds, there was no response and Dodge feared the other man might be unable to overcome the paralysis of fear, but then the opposite door opened and Sadiki crawled inside, likewise keeping his head down.

Dodge put the car in gear, but held the clutch down. The opposing forces had ignored them up to that point, but he knew that as soon as the car started moving, all bets would be off. He lifted his head up, just for an instant, and scanned the courtyard, mentally plotting his route. A sweeping turn would take them to the gate in a matter of seconds, but he had one stop to make first.

He ducked down again and let out the clutch. As the car lurched into motion, he cranked the wheel hard, angling toward the front of the house. The vehicle carved a sharp turn and came up parallel to the porch of the house. There was a jolt as a front tire hit the raised step and then rolled up and over it.

"Hurricane!" he shouted toward the house. "Get in!"

There was soft thump behind them. Dodge glanced up and saw that a hawkman had landed on the gunner's platform, his razor-tipped wings spread wide in preparation for a killing strike. Confined within the car's interior, there was no avoiding it, but Dodge had one last trick left up his sleeve.

As the wings started to come down, Dodge slammed on the brakes. The hawkman pitched headlong, sailing past Dodge and out over the front end of the car, but the killer twisted in midair and, instead of crashing to the paving stones, he lofted into the air, circled around and dropped back down onto the hood of the now-motionless vehicle. The wings rose again, but this time, Dodge was out of tricks.

Then something slammed into the side of the car and everything dissolved into darkness.

Molly gripped the bulkhead and closed her eyes as the bottom fell out of the world. That's how it felt anyway. An experienced airplane pilot, Molly had no qualms about flying, but the dirigible rose straight up like an out of control elevator. The sensation passed after a few seconds, but it was a few more before she dared to open her eyes.

Moments before take-off, Novotny's men had herded her and the other woman into a small compartment at the rear of the cabin. There had been one other occupant, an old man in rumpled clothes, but before introductions could be made, a bell rang and the airship had taken off.

"So. The real Molly Rose Shannon, in the flesh."

Molly opened her eyes and met the other woman's stare. "Does this mean you're done pretending to be me?"

"I was trying to save you," the woman shot back. "If you'd just played along, you and Dodge would be back together."

The harsh words stung, particularly the last part. Molly swallowed. "You're right. I'm sorry. Thanks for trying."

The woman stuck out her hand. "I'm Liz."

Molly shook the proffered hand. "How'd you get mixed up in this, Liz?"

"Mixed up is right," Liz said with a nervous laugh. "I'm the lead writer for the Dodge Dalton serials. I was with Dodge… working with him, I mean… when those birdmen tried to kill him."

Molly sighed. "Another innocent bystander caught up in one of Dodge's adventures. Typical."

She immediately regretted the comment. Maybe Liz was an unwilling participant, but she couldn't lay the blame for everything else at Dodge's feet. He had been on the other side of the world when the Nazis had grabbed her and Hurricane.

Liz raised an eyebrow. "That's not what I would have expected from you."

"You just met me."

"I suppose, but I feel like I've known you for a long time."

"From Dodge's stories." Molly shook her head. "That's not the real me."

"But you are his girlfriend?"

"I don't know what I am anymore."

Liz stared at her in shocked silence for a moment.

"Dodge and I…" Molly shook her head and tried again. "A lot has happened in both our lives. To you, they're just stories, but to me it's all real. The villains are real, the pain and death are real. Now you're caught in it, too.

"This isn't what I wanted," she continued. "These adventures. I wish my father was still here, that Dodge and I could be together, a thousand miles away from all this insanity. But wishing won't change how the world really is. Or get us out of this mess."

"You do know that Dodge is still very much in love with you."

Molly was taken aback, not so much by the frank statement as she was by how obvious it was to this stranger. "Sometimes that's not enough."

Liz turned to the other captive. "What's your story, mister?"

The old man straightened, but before he could answer the sound of gunfire reverberated through the gondola.

"The Nazis are shooting at us!" Liz exclaimed.

"At Novotny," the old man said. "He's as treacherous as a scorpion. Now that he has what he wants, he has no further need of the Nazis."

"What he wants," Molly repeated. "You mean me?"

"My dear, I have no idea who you are or what he wants with you. I am what he wants."

"No offense mister," Liz put in, "But that's not how it looked from where I was standing."

"Hmm." The man took a pipe from his pocket and clamped his teeth down on the stem as he pondered this. "You may be right about that. Perhaps there is more going on here than I realized."

"There most certainly is, Professor Dunn." Novotny strode into the cabin and stopped in front of the old man. "However, that is of no concern to you. Your role in this affair is quite simple. Tell me where to find the Door."

The Door?

A memory came unbidden. *There are other gates—places where the membrane separating realities is weakest. Even now, he searches for the Osiris Gate in the deserts of Egypt.*

Molly's eyes darted from Dunn to Novotny. "You're the Prisoner."

Novotny turned slowly to look at her, his colorless eyes boring into her soul. "He spoke of me. In a dream."

Molly's heart began pounding. "I won't help you."

Novotny laughed softly. "Oh, but you already have."

Liz spoke up. "Buster, I don't think you know who you're messing with here. That's Dodge Dalton's girl."

He turned to her. "Indeed. But who are you? A pretender? I should throw you out the door right now."

"Well ain't you a tough guy, picking on a couple women and an old man. Maybe we should find a puppy for you to kick while you're at it."

"Your friend Dalton has proven more even resourceful than I anticipated," Novotny said, dismissing the jibe. "But he cannot help you now. His bones will never leave this desert."

"Wanna bet?"

Novotny ignored her, returning his attention to Molly. "He speaks to you in dreams."

She knew he wasn't talking about Dodge any more.

"And you speak to him. The link between you connects this world with the next." Novotny laughed softly, then turned back to Dunn. "The Door, professor. Where is it?"

"Don't tell him," Molly pleaded, gripping Dunn's arm. "You were with Doc Newcombe, weren't you? He must have told you what will happen if that Door is opened."

"Professor Dunn also knows what will happen to his daughter if he refuses," Novotny said.

A strange sad smile touched Dunn's lips. "Your threats are empty, Novotny. You can't touch her."

For the first time since entering the cabin, Novotny seemed nonplussed. "You cannot hide her from me. If you do not lead me to the Door, I will turn the world upside down to find her."

"You can try, but you won't find her."

Novotny's dead eyes suddenly came alive. "Your daughter found the Door. She has passed through. That's why I couldn't find her."

Molly saw the truth of it in Dunn's face

"Your daughter has passed through the Door," Novotny said again, smiling in triumph. "She is trapped in the Realm of Osiris. Take me there and I will see to it that you are reunited with her. It is the only way you will ever see her again."

"Don't do it," Molly said. "You don't know what's at stake."

Dunn smiled his sad smile again then looked away from her. "It's at Ain Della."

"Ain Della?" Novotny said. "The Hidden Valley. I searched it. There's nothing there."

"I thought so as well, but my Fiona was evidently more thorough than you and I put together." Dunn took something from his pocket and held it up for display. It looked to Molly like a piece from a chess set.

"A djed amulet?" Novotny said. He reached a hand out as if to take it from Dunn, but then stopped. "I remember...." His voice trailed off as if the memory had slipped away and he drew his hand back, empty.

"This is the key that unlocks the door between day and night," Dunn said, reverently. "When we arrive at the Hidden Valley, you will see."

"If your daughter used this to open the Door, how did it come into your possession?"

"My manservant Sadiki was with her. He returned it to me, along with the news of her fate."

"If you are lying to me..." Novotny let the threat hang in the air, then spun on his heel, exiting the room as abruptly as he had entered.

Even through the closed door, Molly could hear him shouting. "Sound the recall alarm. Set course for Ain Della."

She turned to Dunn again. "He's lying. And if he succeeds in opening that Door, none of us will survive."

"Don't worry," Dunn said cryptically. "He won't."

The journey was unexpectedly brief. Less than half an hour after leaving Farafra, the airship nosed down and cut its engines. A few minutes later, the gondola bumped down on the desert floor and the three captives were dragged out into the chilly night.

They were joined by a contingent of hawkmen, who had exchanged their wings and black garments, for simple Bedouin robes, rifles and flashlights, and Novotny, who now sported a faded duster.

"Which way, professor?" he demanded impatiently.

"It will be harder to locate in the dark," Dunn said. "Can't we wait until sunrise?"

Novotny glared at the old man for a moment, then bent close to Liz. He reached out one glove hand, tracing the line of her jaw with a finger. "Professor Dunn. As I can no longer persuade you to help me for the sake of your daughter, perhaps I need to find some other means of exerting…" He looked back to Dunn. "Leverage."

Dunn threw his hands up. "Leave her alone. I told you I would take you there." He looked around, searching for landmarks. "There are old some old ruins around here."

"Those date to Roman times. Far too recent."

"Did it occur to you that the Roman might have chosen to establish their outpost on that spot for a reason?"

"They built over an existing ruin?"

"Two and a half millennia ago, the Persian king Cambyses sent an army to conquer the Oracle of Amun. They made it as far as this oasis, and then vanished. Fifty thousand men. Gone."

"I know the story," Novotny said, irritably. "They were buried in a sandstorm."

"That is the story," Dunn agreed. "But no trace of them has ever been found."

"You believe they passed through the Door?"

Dunn shrugged. "Until recently, I would not have given any credence to the story. But if the Door is real, then is it not also possible that the Oracle knew the secret of how to open it, how to use its power to defeat the army of Cambyses?"

Novotny shook his head. "I searched the site thoroughly. The Door is not there."

Dunn held up the djed amulet. "You didn't have the key."

Novotny considered this for a moment, then gestured for the party to follow.

The ruins were little more than crumbling mud brick walls, but a recently excavated trench revealed a narrow opening into a chamber underneath the limestone foundation of the old structure.

"This is it." Novotny seemed almost to tremble with anticipation.

Molly shook with a different emotion. She could feel the presence of the Door—the Gate, as her father had called it. A place where the membrane separating one world from the next was dangerously thin.

You must escape. Before he finds the Gate.

Escape? How?

"Here," Novotny called out, shining a flashlight on the floor of a carved semi-circular chamber. "These are your daughter's footprints, Professor."

The trail ended abruptly at the far wall.

"Dead end," Liz muttered, then winced. "Uh, sorry. That was the wrong thing to say."

Novotny approached the wall and began scrutinizing every crack and pockmark. After a few minutes of this, he turned, a triumphant look on his face. His flashlight shone on a small hole, a pockmark in the stone, barely bigger than Molly's thumb. "Now, professor. I will take that key."

Molly suddenly felt very cold.

Dunn hesitated a moment, then held out the djed amulet. Novotny plucked it from his fingers and held it up like the prize from a box of Cracker Jack. "Rejoice, professor. Soon you will be reunited with your daughter."

He turned back, reverently bringing the amulet close to the hole, and then with a flourish, slid the ancient key into the keyhole. "Behold! The Door of Osiris opens!"

Nothing happened.

"Well that was kind of anticlimactic," Liz remarked.

For the first time since being captured by the Nazis, Molly felt a glimmer of hope. *Maybe it's not too late.*

Novotny stared at the wall for several seconds then pounded his fists on it in frustration. He whirled around to face Dunn. "This is the Door. I know it. Why is nothing happening?"

Dunn spread his hands. "I did what you asked. It's not my fault."

Novotny continued to stare at him with his dead eyes, then he abruptly turned back to the wall, pulled the djed amulet from the hole. He brought it close to his face, inspecting with closely in the beam of the flashlight for a moment. Then he flung it at Dunn.

"A cheap forgery," he snarled. "Where is the real key?"

"I don't understand. I was certain that was it." Dunn spread his hands in a gesture of innocence, but Molly could see a gleam of triumph in his eyes.

He knew it was a fake all along, she realized.

Novotny realized this as well. "It's still with your servant." He shook his head angrily. "You've accomplished nothing with this delay, professor. I will search the bodies at Farafra until I find the key, and then I will tear down the walls between the worlds. You however, will not live to see it."

Novotny drew a pistol from beneath his duster, aimed it at Dunn's heart, and fired three shots in quick succession. The reports were astonishingly loud in the close quarters of the chamber. The impact drove the old man back into the arms of Molly and Liz. He didn't appear to weigh much but he bore them both to the ground.

Molly, who had once studied to be a doctor, almost reflexively tried to stanch the flow of blood from the old man's chest, she knew the wound was mortal. Dunn's lips were moving, trying to say something with his last breath. Molly couldn't hear anything over the ringing in her ears, but she understood all the same.

Save Fiona.

Then Novotny's men grabbed her arms and dragged her and Liz away, leaving Dunn to die alone in the dark.

CHAPTER 15— DODGE OF THE DESERT

The shockwave knocked the wind out of Dodge, which was probably for the best since the air was so full of dust and grit that he probably wouldn't have been able to breathe it in anyway. The concussive force of the explosion pushed the car away from the porch like it had been T-boned by a delivery truck. Chunks of debris pounded the side of the car, denting the fenders and stripping the paint. More fragments whizzed through the air overhead, but miraculously, none of it got through to the two figures crouched down inside the vehicle. Aside from being momentarily dazed, Dodge weathered the explosion pretty well.

The same could not be said for the hawkman who had been perched on the front of the car. The blast had completely erased him from existence. But any relief Dodge might have felt at this unexpected reprieve was dampened by the realization that the explosion had come from inside the big house.

Where Hurricane, Newcombe and Wittgenstein had taken cover.

Amazingly, the car was still running, and when he unthinkingly lifted his feet off the clutch and brake pedals, it gave a violent lurch and stalled. He barely noticed.

He opened his mouth to shout, but no sound came out. He tried again, working his mouth like a fish out of water until his shocked lungs finally drew in some of the thick air.

"Hurricane!" He clambered over the crumpled side door and picked his way through the litter toward the gaping hole where the front door of the house had been. "Doc! Hurricane!"

The spacious front room was unrecognizable. Chunks of plaster and broken mud bricks littered the floor along with other large pieces of wreckage that might have once been furniture.

"Dodge!" It was Newcombe's voice, the shout strong even though it sounded barely louder than a whisper as it filtered through to Dodge's muddled head.

"Doc?" He looked around, trying to find his friend.

"Up here!" Newcombe's waving hand, hanging down through a gaping hole in the ceiling, finally caught his attention. Newcombe and Wittgenstein, looking a little rattled but otherwise no worse for wear, peered down through the hole at him.

"Where's Hurricane?"

Newcombe shook his head uncertainly, but Wittgenstein's finger shot out, pointing to a Hurricane Hurley sized heap of rubble against the far wall. "There!"

Something was stirring beneath it.

"Get down here," Dodge shouted, then rushed over and began carefully removing the largest pieces of debris. A few seconds later, one of Hurricane's massive arms shot out the pile and, far less delicately, swept the rest of the rubble onto the floor.

"Damned Kraut potato mashers," he roared, sitting up. He was covered in dust, with dark streaks on his face and around his ears that might have been blood caked with grime. "They're making those things stronger than they used to. Either that, or I'm getting old."

Dodge was only a little bit astonished to find his old friend alive and kicking. If anyone could survive a blast like that, it was Hurricane. Even so, he couldn't hide a smile of relief.

"What's that?" Hurricane shouted.

"I didn't say anything."

"You're gonna have to speak up. I can't hear a bless things."

Dodge grinned and pointed to the door.

Outside, the shooting had stopped. Dodge poked his head out cautiously and saw at least a dozen bodies, mostly SS troopers, but there were a few hawkmen scattered among them like fallen angels. If anyone still lived, they were either unconscious or playing possum. He watched and waited for a full minute to make sure the skies were clear of hawkmen, before leading the mad dash to the battered but still functional vehicle. He got it running again and, when everyone was on board, headed through the gate.

"Sadiki. You know where Novotny is going?"

The other man nodded. "An oasis called Ain Della. It is seventy-five kilometers north of Farafra, but... Novotny still has an army. And an airship. You will never be able to defeat him."

"Never say never," Hurricane rumbled softly. "Especially not when you're talking to Dodge Dalton."

Dodge threw him a grateful nod. Evidently, the big man's hearing was returning. But Sadiki wasn't wrong. Novotny had his winged killers and a distinct high-altitude advantage. And he had a head start.

But Novotny also had Molly and Liz. And if he found what he was looking for at Ain Della, it would mean the end of the world. Whether or not they could beat him was an irrelevant concern. They had no choice but to try.

Wilhelm Kaufmann awoke with a gasp. He had barely been clinging to consciousness before the explosion, and the concussive blast had been more than enough to send him over the edge, into blissful oblivion. As the shock wore off however, the weight of the debris that had collapsed onto him, pressing down on his chest, suffocating him, dragged him back to wakeful-ness. His eyes flew open and he began struggling out the rubble like a chick fighting its way out of the egg.

When he was able to breathe again, he lay there for a moment, resting from his exertions. His body ached from bruises too numerous to count, and he knew the aches he felt would only multiply in the hours and days to come, but he also knew his injuries were not life threatening. It took a few more seconds for his muddled brain to begin making sense of what had just happened.

"Novotny," he whispered, spitting the name out like a curse.

If the ominous silence was any indication, the battle had already ended and his forces had been overwhelmed. Massacred. There might still be a few survivors in the house or outside, but if he was to repay Novotny's treach-ery, he would need to radio for reinforcements.

That fool Himmler would not dare refuse the urgent request. It was his fault after all. He had trusted Novotny, been enticed by the promise of mystical power, and allowed the resources of the Third Reich to be subvert-ed by an enemy who had betrayed them at the first opportunity. And if revenge wasn't a sweet enough enticement, there was always the Black Sun. Novotny would not have so lightly dismissed his partnership with the Nazi regime unless that prize was almost within his grasp.

Once he destroyed Novotny, the Black Sun would be his to command.

Energized by the possibilities, he got to his feet and headed for the radio room.

As they drove across the desert, Dodge compared notes with his compan-ions. After describing the various paths that had brought them all to Farafra Oasis, the discussion turned to the nature of the enemy. Wittgenstein had a few valuable insights, though separating them from his esoteric ramblings felt a little like panning for gold.

Hurricane summed it up succinctly. "So this Novotny is just the latest edition of the Prisoner. He needs Molly to distract the Padre so he can bring back those pillar thingies. He sent the Nazis to round us up, and then went after you because he knew you would throw a monkey wrench in the works."

"Pretty much."

"Well, let's not disappoint him."

"It may be more complicated than that," Wittgenstein said. "I believe that the dreams Miss Shannon was having, and which brought her to me, are indicative of a problem of much greater magnitude."

"Meaning?"

"Meaning that the fate of... well, everything... may hang in the balance."

"So what else is new?" Hurricane said.

"Miss Shannon has a psychical link to her father, a link that transcends universes. If I understand the situation correctly, her father—the man Mr. Hurley calls 'Padre'—is acting as a sort of gatekeeper. This Novotny fellow, or the Prisoner as you call him, enslaved entities from beyond that gate."

"That's right," Newcombe supplied. "They're imprisoned inside pillars of indestructible adamantine."

"Indestructible?" Wittgenstein mused. "Hyperbolic acid might do the trick. One of my colleagues concocted it. An acid that can melt through anything."

"Ridiculous," Newcombe said. "There's no such thing."

"I told my colleague as much, but he insisted. He even brought a flask of it over to show me."

"If it could melt through anything, then no flask could hold it."

Wittgenstien tapped his nose and grinned. "It's a classic paradox. One warrior has a spear that can pierce any shield. The other has a shield that can break any spear. Who will win?"

"You're saying there is a way to destroy adamantine?" Dodge asked.

"This is not my field of expertise, but it stands to reason that anything which can be created can be destroyed. So 'indestructible' is a relative term. As relative indestructibility increases, the amount of force required to destroy it also increases. Tell me, Dr. Newcombe, how was this Prisoner able to enslave these extradimensional beings in adamantine in the first place?"

"He used their own power against them."

"Ah, so something unbound by the limitations of natural laws. An externality. A different question then. Where did adamantine originate?"

"Eddington and Bethe have proposed that all elements are produced by a process called nuclear fusion which takes place in stars. Simple elements combine to form new compounds, releasing a great deal of energy in the process. Eventually those stars reach a certain critical mass and explode as supernovae. The heavier elements are blown out across the universe. I would theorize that perhaps a meteorite of adamantine, produced in just such an event, found its way to earth at some point in the distant past."

"Ah, so a furnace as hot as an exploding sun would be required to destroy the adamantine. These... pillar entities, I believe is what you called them... must possess the power to create such a fire, true? What prevents them from doing so?"

"The Padre," Hurricane said. "He took charge of 'em. It's like havin' a tiger by the tail, but as long as he's holdin' on to 'em, they're stuck."

"I gathered as much. That's why Miss Shannon's link to the Padre is so problematic. It allows him to speak with her from the threshold of the door between worlds, but it also leaves him vulnerable...through her."

"You're saying that Novotny is going to hurt Molly in order to hurt the Padre?" Dodge said.

"The connection goes both ways. Novotny will attempt to use Miss Shannon to weaken the Padre so that he may take control of these entities. But, to borrow Mr. Hurley's metaphor, when the Padre let's go of the tiger's tail, it may turn on them both. The entities will seize on that moment to tear down the walls that imprison them."

"Releasing enough energy to destroy the entire planet," Newcombe finished.

"If Novotny is the Prisoner," Hurricane said, "He's gotta know that might happen."

"He does know," Dodge said. "Or he did. Thousands of years ago, those entities drove him mad, trying to convince him to release them. He almost gave in. That's how he ended up trapped at the Outpost in Antarctica. I think they're whispering to him again, tricking him into doing this."

"So, we have to save Molly in order to save the world," Hurricane said. "Hell, like we needed another reason. But what's he waitin' for?"

"This Door of Osiris that Miss Fiona Dunn discovered must be another point of intersection between the worlds. That is where he will go."

"Sadiki," Newcombe said. "The amulet? Do you still have it?"

There was a rustle of fabric as Sadiki searched his pockets and then held up a small object that glistened in the moonlight.

"Dodge, we're in luck," Newcombe went on. "Novotny needs this amulet in order to open the Door. We have plenty of time to figure this out."

"Molly and Liz might disagree," Dodge said. "And it won't take long for Novotny to figure it out and come looking for us."

"Maybe we should get rid of it," Hurricane said. "Toss it into the deepest part of the ocean."

"We can't do that," Newcombe said, quickly. "Fiona is trapped on the other side. We have to rescue her."

"He's right," Dodge said. "We'll rescue Fiona and then close that Door. Permanently. Then we'll deal with Novotny."

"How?"

"Sadiki said this place is seventy-five kilometers away," Dodge said. "We should be able to cover that distance in an hour. That's how long we've got to come up with a plan."

It quickly became apparent that they would have a great deal more time to formulate a plan than Dodge had originally estimated. The first warning sign came just a few minutes later, with a whine of protest from the engine, which soon became a persistent knocking sound. The smell of burning oil and hot metal stung Dodge's eyes and nostrils, and a check of the temperature gaze confirmed his worst fears. They were overheating.

It wasn't hard to guess the cause. In the fury of battle, something—a stray bullet or maybe more than one, or possibly the explosion that had blasted the side out of the house—had damaged the radiator. Dodge made the hard decision to turn back, but it was already too late. A few minutes later the engine's death rattle intensified and then with grinding lurch, it seized up and car came to a stop in the middle of the open desert.

Dodge pounded the steering wheel with his fists in impotent frustration, then turned to his companions. "Now what?"

He couldn't see their faces clearly in the moonlit darkness, but the ensuing silence was answer enough. They were looking to him for answers.

"Sadiki, how much further is it?"

"I do not know. Perhaps another forty or fifty kilometers."

"Thirty miles," Hurricane said. "That's a bit further than I feel like walking."

"It is doubtful that we could survive such a journey across the desert," Sadiki added. "Not in our current state."

"Well we can't sit here and wait for a tow truck," Dodge said. "Farafra is closer. Maybe ten miles."

Hurricane let out a thoughtful hum. "I feel I should point out that we may not receive the warmest welcome there."

"We don't exactly have a choice."

"There are Bedouin encampments on the outskirts of the settlement," Sadiki said. "We may be able to find assistance there. Camels. Water and food for the desert crossing."

"Camels," Hurricane snorted in disgust. "Walking doesn't sound so bad after all."

A hasty search of the vehicle yielded a single half-filled coconut-shaped canteen, a discarded Luger pistol with three rounds in the magazine, and not much else in the way of desert survival gear. The pistol wouldn't be much use if they found themselves in a firefight—Hurricane had that covered with his .50 caliber hand-cannons—but Dodge jammed the gun into his belt, just in case. Sadiki tore fabric from the vehicle's seat covers to fashion head-cloths for each of them, and then they headed south, following their tire tracks.

Sadiki set a slow but purposeful pace, with frequent rest breaks even though Dodge was impatient to keep moving. The night air was cool but the exertion nevertheless left Dodge feeling parched. At each break, they allowed themselves a small sip from the canteen, but split five ways, Dodge knew it wouldn't be long before the container was bone dry.

As they were just about to resume the trek following a stop, Sadiki stiffened in alarm. "Quickly, we must hide."

"Hide?" Hurricane gestured to the flat open landscape. "Where do you propose we do that?"

Sadiki answered by dropping to his knees and burrowing into the sand like a dog searching for a bone. Dodge shrugged and followed the man's example. A few seconds later, he heard the distant drone of an engine. Novotny's dirigible, cruising through the sky somewhere above them, returning to the Nazi compound at Farafra Oasis to search for the amulet. It was unlikely that the villain would spot them at night and from a distance, but it was a chance they couldn't take.

As the hum grew louder, Dodge scrambled into the shallow hole he'd dug and began scooping sand over himself. The engine noise was everywhere, and insidious hum that set his teeth on edge. When he looked up, there was a black emptiness where the stars should have been directly above his head.

Had they been spotted?

He lay there for a minute. Two minutes. Five.

Something was crawling against his skin. On his arms, his legs, his face…

No, it's just my imagination, he told himself. But what if it wasn't? What if it was one of the regions deadly Deathstalker scorpions?

He clenched his teeth, and forced himself to remain statue still.

After a few more minutes, the engine hum began to fade and then all was quiet.

"All clear," Sadiki said, rising from his shallow grave.

Dodge jumped up and started shaking the sand out of his clothing. Newcombe and Wittgenstein did the same. Hurricane just laughed.

There were no scorpions, no creepy crawlies. It had all been his imagination.

"It won't take him long to figure out that the amulet's not there," Hurricane said.

"Or us," Dodge said. "These tire tracks will lead him right to us. Sadiki…"

"Yes, I know." Their guide studied the landscape for several seconds, then pointed in a different direction. "This way."

Twenty or so minutes later, Sadiki called another halt.

"At this rate, we should get there sometime next year," Hurricane grumbled.

Dodge nodded and approached their guide. "Sadiki, we can't afford any more rest stops."

"No a rest stop," Sadiki whispered. "We are being watched."

"Are you sure?" Dodge resisted the urge to draw the Luger from his belt. "By whom?"

As if in answer, a voice rang out from the darkness. The utterance was short, and in what Dodge could only assume was Arabic. Sadiki answered back at somewhat greater length in the same language. Most of it was incomprehensible, but Dodge heard his own name mentioned. After Sadiki finished, there was a long pause and then a pair of robed figures appeared before them and beckoned them to follow. The men were just silhouettes in the moonlight, but Dodge could see the distinctive outline of rifles slung over their shoulders, barrels pointing skyward.

"These are the Bedouins I told you of," Sadiki explained. "We may enter their camp."

"You sure we can trust these fellas?" Hurricane asked.

"No," Sadiki admitted. "But we are at their mercy."

"We'll see about that."

"Hurricane," Dodge admonished. "Let's try asking nicely before we start breaking things."

They were escorted a short distance to a circle of tents that, in the moonlight, might have been mistaken for sand dunes, but there was no mistaking the smell of cooking meat and spices rising from the encampment. One of their men disappeared into the largest tent, emerging a few moments later with a lantern in hand and accompanied by another Bedouin—an immense man with a bushy salt-and-pepper beard that reached down to his chest.

More lights appeared all around them, revealing dozens of Bedouins, their faces hidden behind heavy veils.

"Dodge," Hurricane murmured. "This isn't good."

"Could they be working with the Nazis?" Newcombe whispered.

The bearded man took a few steps closer, scrutinizing them one by one. He had neither lantern nor weapon, but there was something in his hand. It was a piece of paper, though in the scant light, it was impossible to tell what, if anything, was written on it. He finally brought his gaze back to Dodge.

"You," he said, in a booming voice, "are Dodge Dalton?"

"He speaks English," Newcombe said, unnecessarily. "Is that a good sign?"

"That's right," Dodge said, matching the fellow's intent stare. "And these are my friends, Hurricane Hurley, Doctor Findlay Newcombe, Professor Ludvig Wittgenstein, and Sadiki, our guide."

The bearded man took another step forward, then threw his arms around Dodge. "Dodge Dalton," he cried out. "Captain Falcon. Newspaper hero of the world!"

He released Dodge and stepped back, waving the paper in front of Dodge's face. It was a yellowed piece of newsprint, emblazoned with the masthead of The Clarion, the New York tabloid where Dodge had gotten his start.

"You honor our tents with your presence," the Bedouin said. "Come, we must celebrate."

As Dodge was dragged into the tent he looked back at Newcombe and grinned. "That," he said, "is a good sign."

The feast was sumptuous, though Dodge was hard pressed to identify any of the dishes. As they dined, the Bedouin explained how he had, as a young boy traveled with T.E. Lawrence and learned to speak and read English, before returning to his *asha'ir*—a word that seemed to correspond to "tribe" or "clan"—to take his place as their leader, or *Sheikh*, To maintain and sharpen his linguistic skills, the Sheikh made it a point to acquire English language books and newspapers whenever their nomadic wanderings brought them to civilization, which was how he had discovered *The Adventures of Captain Falcon*. The stories had been a big hit with the rest of the clan.

Under any other circumstances, Dodge would have welcomed the adoration of fans, but with Novotny prowling the desert searching for the key that would open the Door between worlds—and end at least one of them permanently—there was little time to enjoy the hospitality of the Bedouins. At the first opportunity, Dodge explained their plight.

"We can't stay here," he finished. "Just coming here puts you all in danger."

The Sheikh scowled. "I know of this man who flies a skyship. He lured many of our sons away, enticing them to follow the false gods of the ancients. He gave them wings made of knives and turned them against the *asha'ir*."

"I saw this," Sadiki said. "Before Professor Dunn and I came to find you, Dr. Newcombe. The hawkmen attacked a group of Bedouins not far from here."

"We need to get to the oasis of Ain Della as soon as possible," Dodge went on. "There's something there that Novotny wants. We have to stop him from getting it. Unfortunately, our car broke down."

"If you would destroy this man, I would help you even if you were not Dodge Dalton." The Sheik got to his feet. "Come."

As they followed the Bedouin, Dodge tried to explain his plan. "We need to sneak back into Farafra and find a working car."

"Farafra is crawling with Nazis," the Sheikh pointed out.

"That's the least of our worries," Hurricane said. "Novotny is there, too."

The Bedouin stopped for a moment and looked back, but then shook his head and gestured another tent. "We will ride for Ain Della."

"Ride?" Hurricane groaned. "I hate camels."

The Bedouin grinned behind his beard and threw back the tent flap. The light from his lamp was reflected back, in a myriad of brilliant starburst, from the polished chrome accents of, not one but five motorcycles. "Who said anything about camels?"

On the day that she boarded Greyhound bus bound for California, Elizabeth Sansom's father had angrily predicted that she would come crawling back to him, desperate and helpless. Liz in turn had made a solemn vow that she would never allow herself to be either desperate or helpless. Her stubborn resolve had helped her survive the snakepit of Hollywood that had devoured so many others before her. She had endured long days and lean weeks, and never begged for help or traded her dignity for easy money. Even when things seemed hopeless, she never allowed herself to feel helpless.

Until now.

After killing Professor Dunn, Novotny had rushed them back to the airship and given the command to return to Farafra, dashing Liz's hopes that Dodge and the others might have survived the initial massacre. If Dodge was still alive, Novotny would hunt him down and kill him, and then there wouldn't be any reason for the villain to keep her alive.

Molly must have noticed her fighting back tears because she threw her arms around Liz and hugged her tight.

Liz returned the embrace even though she knew the situation was completely hopeless. "Do you think Dodge is still...?"

Molly's arms went slack as if some of the life had gone out of her. "I'm sure he is," she said, her voice oddly flat. "He's survived a lot worse."

"I'm sorry," Liz said.

"Whatever for?"

"I don't know. I guess that things are so… That you and Dodge…" Liz realized that she was just making a bad situation worse. "Never mind. I'm going to shut up now."

"That's probably a good idea." Molly replied. Then her tone softened. "I'm sorry, I shouldn't have said that. It's just…you can't possibly understand."

"Talking about it might help."

"I don't think anything can help," Molly said miserably.

"Can't hurt."

"No, I suppose it can't."

And then she began to talk. The story poured out of her. From her research, Liz knew that Molly had spent most of her life in Africa, at a Congo river mission, raised by a dour Catholic priest. She had probably never had a good old-fashioned girl-to-girl talk.

Liz was surprised to learn that Dodge was Molly's first crush, though in hindsight it seemed obvious. When Molly had lost her adopted dad, Father Nathan Hobbs, her world had come apart. Instead of drawing closer to Dodge, she had pulled away, knowing that one day, she would lose him too. But instead of finding solace in her new calling, providing medical care to the Untouchables—the lowly outcastes living in the slums of India—her worst nightmares had come true. Her dad's ghost—maybe he wasn't a ghost exactly, but close enough—had returned to haunted her dreams, and now Novotny was threatening her life.

"He wants to use me against my dad," Molly explained. "That's the worst part. Novotny is going to use me to destroy the world."

No wonder the poor girl is all mixed up, she thought. Love was hard enough without having to constantly deal with life and death. "Never give up hope," she told Molly.

"This isn't one of your movies, Liz. Not every story has a happy ending."

"This one will. We just haven't gotten to it yet."

As if to prove her wrong—or maybe prove her right—Novotny stormed into the cabin.

"Uh, oh," Liz said, feeling a little of her customary spunk returning. "He doesn't look happy."

"Dodge got away," Molly said. "Didn't he?"

"For all the good it will do him," Novotny snarled. We'll hunt him down and then he will watch as I have you torn limb from limb."

"You don't have to hunt him" Molly said. "He'll find you. And he'll beat you. Just like he did last time."

Novotny, quivering with rage, took a step closer. "Silence."

"You know it's true. He'll beat you. He'll beat you every time."

What's she doing? Liz thought. *If she keeps this up, he'll kill her.*

As if on cue, Novotny's hand shot out, closing around Molly's throat. "Silence!" he roared, lifting her into the air.

Her lips moved but no sound could get past the chokehold. She clutched at his fingers, but could not pry them loose. Her face went purple and then her eyes rolled back in her head.

"Stop it!" Liz pleaded. "You're killing her! She's no good to you dead."

No good to him dead, Liz thought. *Oh, Molly. No....*

Novotny must have realized it too. The rage behind his eyes died and he opened his hand, allowing the unconscious girl to fall to the deck. "No," he said. "Death will not save your world."

Time and the blowing desert wind had sculpted the White Desert into a wonderland of bizarre chalk formations that rose like giant mushrooms from the snow-colored sand. In the moonlight, the towering rocks looked even more surreal, an army of colossal statues, half-buried in the sand but slowly coming to life.

A harbinger of what they would find when they reached Ain Della and the Door of Osiris.

Seated astride one of the Sheikh's prized Brough Superior motorcycles, and alone with his thoughts, Dodge could not help but contemplate the dire consequences of failure. If they did not stop Novotny—the latest incarnation of the ancient Prisoner—this long night would go on forever.

Fortunately, the ride was relatively short. The motorcycles devoured the distance between the Bedouin camp and the oasis.

Dodge, with Wittgenstein riding behind him, pulled up alongside the Sheikh, who was riding double with one of his sons, and killed the engine.

"Magnificent, are they not?" The Sheikh boomed.

Dodge surveyed the ruin—the walls were worn down like an old man's teeth—wondering what the Bedouin found so impressive.

"The Rolls Royce of motorcycles, each one handmade by George Brough himself."

"I may have to order one myself," Hurricane remarked as he dismounted his, which was equipped with a sidecar into which Newcombe and Sadiki were crammed.

"It is said that Ned buys a new one every year."

"The motorcycles," Dodge said, nodding. The Sheikh evidently was unaware that his hero, T.E. "Ned" Lawrence, had died a few years earlier from injuries sustained in a crash while riding one of his beloved custom-built motorcycles. Dodge decided not be the bearer of that bad news.

Sadiki extricated himself from the sidecar and moved hesitantly toward the remains of the ancient building. "This is where…" His voice trailed off, the memory evidently too painful.

He had told them all the story, how he and Fiona Dunn had excavated under the old ruin, found and opened a door into a strange otherwhere, and how he had been forced to leave her behind. He had not been able to adequately explain why Fiona had been trapped, and this was a detail that

Dodge found especially troubling, but Sadiki was already inconsolable and Dodge knew further questioning would be futile.

"Time has no meaning in the universe beyond the Door," Newcombe said, trying as much to reassure himself as Sadiki. "For Fiona, it may be that only a few seconds have passed."

Or a thousand years, Dodge thought, recalling his own experience with a similar phenomenon in Antarctica.

"Time may not mean a thing in there," Hurricane said, "But it's tickin' away something fierce out here. Let's get a move on."

"This is a place of ill omen," the Sheikh said, gesturing to the ruins. "My sons and I will not accompany you into the belly of the earth, but we will remain here and watch over you."

"You've done more than enough," Dodge told him. "You should return to your people. If Novotny tracks us to your camp, they could all be in danger."

The Sheikh gave a fierce nod. "I will leave motorcycles. Enough for you and your friends when you rescue you them. I do not doubt that you will. Only promise me two things. You must return them to me if you can. And you must write about me in your next adventure."

Dodge clasped his hand. "It's a deal."

Sadiki led them to the trench and showed them the passage the beneath the ruin. As they filed into it behind him, Dodge thought he heard a strange hum in the air. He thought it might be the whine of the distant motorcycle engines—the Sheikh and his sons departing—but it seemed to grow louder as they moved deeper underground.

"Does anyone else hear that?"

"It comes from beyond the Door," Sadiki said. "It will only get louder as we... No!"

Sadiki let out a wail of grief and rushed ahead, the droning sound all but forgotten. Dodge stepped through and saw the servant bent over the body of an old man, who lay slumped against one wall.

"It's Professor Dunn," Newcombe gasped. He pushed past Dodge and rushed to Sadiki's side. The scientist touched the old man's neck, feeling for a pulse, then let his head fall forward. The old man's pallor was evidence of his fate; the bloody holes in his chest confirmed it.

Newcombe looked away, then picked something up off the floor and held it up. It was a djed amulet, similar to the one Sadiki carried. "I've seen this before. It was in the office of the Commandant in Port Said."

"The Professor pulled a switcheroo on Novotny," Hurricane surmised.

"He knew that Sadiki had the real key and that we would come here," Dodge said. He stepped forward and laid a hand on the servant's shoulder. "He sacrificed himself to give us the time to get here so that you could rescue Fiona."

Sadiki wiped a sleeve across his eyes and nodded. "Yes. You are right." He got to his feet and took the authentic amulet from his pocket, and as he did, the persistent hum seemed to grow louder. The floor began to vibrate beneath their feet, particles of sand dancing and jumping as if alive. As Sadiki moved closer to the opposite wall, the sound intensified and the particles began moving, forming a pattern of concentric circles on the stone floor.

"Well I'll be," Hurricane muttered.

"Chladni figures," Newcombe exclaimed. "I've seen these before. In my laboratory. They're caused by resonance frequencies. Different tones create different patterns in particles of fine sand. They're quite amazing really."

"Is that all they do, doc?"

Sadiki answered for him. "No. It is not. Let me show you."

He took another step forward, holding the amulet out before him like a lantern to guide the way. The stone wall began to shimmer, rippling like the surface of a pond.

"Stop!" Dodge said.

Sadiki froze.

Dodge crossed the chamber and reached out to take the amulet from Sadiki's hand. "Stay here. All of you."

"Dodge," Hurricane said, his low voice oddly harmonizing with the insistent droning sound. "You can't do it alone."

"I can. I'm the only one who can. Beyond that door, reality loses all meaning. We'll get separated, lost in our own nightmares. Just like at the Outpost."

Hurricane stared back at him for a moment, then nodded slowly. "Yeah, I reckon you're right. Be careful in there."

Dodge answered with a nod of his own. He didn't say what he was thinking. Careful wasn't going to cut it. The only way to save Fiona, to save the world, was to throw caution to the wind and do something completely insane.

He closed his fingers over the amulet, and stepped through the wall.

The soldiers marched toward the entrance to the temple, brandishing their machine guns in anticipation of a battle with whatever unholy creatures guarded the treasure within, and Dodge Dalton marched beside them.

"Hold your ground," shouted a voice from behind the column. Dodge recognized Kaufmann's voice and thick Teutonic accent. "The Black Sun is almost within our grasp."

Dodge glanced surreptitiously to the side, past the formation, past the tripod mounted camera, and saw Liz, standing next to the director, a look of eager anticipation on her face.

This was the big climax, the capstone of Black Legion serial, in which the stalwart hero, disguised as an enemy stormtrooper, snuck into the Temple of Osiris and snatched the prize out from under the nose of the Nazi villain.

The story was as contrived as the painted papier-mache columns of the temple set.

Artistic license, Liz had told him. *The audience won't care. They'll be too busy watching movie magic happen on the screen.*

Movie magic, he thought, hiding a smile from the cameras. *Illusion and trickery.*

It relied as much on the audience's willing suspension of disbelief as it did the plausibility of the construct. People saw what they wanted to see, whether it was on the silver screen, or in the strange dreamworld that lay on the other side of the Osiris Door.

What's Kaufmann doing here?

"Eyes front," Hurricane muttered beside him. "We need to get this in one take or Novotny's going to jump down our throats."

The idle thought slipped away. Hurricane was right. Film stock wasn't cheap and time was money, as Novotny was all too fond of pointing out. The last time Dodge ruined a take, Novotny had turned his hawkmen loose to eviscerate Dodge.

Novotny.

Kaufmann.

The names nagged at the back of Dodge's mind as he drew closer to the temple entrance. Up close, the decorations looked woefully amateurish and hasty. Had the set designer had copied them from a photograph of a real Egyptian temple or simply made them up. He wondered what they meant. A curse perhaps? Death and madness to all who enter?

Novotny.

Kaufmann.

Liz.

Molly.

Where's Molly?

A shout went up, followed by the pop-pop of a dozen prop guns, and the soldiers in front of Dodge scattered, revealing the monstrosities emerging from the shadowy depths of the temple. Mummies. Dozens of them. Hundreds. Withered corpses, wrapped in rotting bandages, shambling forward with claw-like hands outstretched.

Movie magic.

Their wailing filled the air, a ghastly familiar droning sound.

Like when Sadiki opened the Osiris Door...

"Let's go!" Hurricane roared, charging headlong into the fray.

His powerful fists knocked the mummies aside like bowling pins, but for every one he took down, three more swarmed in to take their place. In a matter of seconds, the big man was buried under an avalanche of the undead. More mummies poured from the temple entrance, rolling over Hurricane like a tidal wave.

Newcombe grabbed Dodge's arm. "We'll never get through them. We have to find another way in."

Dodge glanced over at the scientist, trying to hide his surprise. He had forgotten that Newcombe was in the film.

"There is no other way," he said. "We have to go through them. We have to get the Black Sun."

From the corner of his eye, he saw Liz flash a big grin. He had nailed his line.

I didn't forget.

This isn't real.

The air around Liz began to ripple like a desert mirage, and in an instant she was gone, along with the cameras and crew.

They were never there. It was just an illusion. Like movie magic.

He wasn't in a soundstage on the Republic Pictures backlot. He was in Egypt, in the Temple of Osiris. The real temple, not a cheap papier-mache set.

He had passed through the Door. The djed amulet was still in his clenched in his hand.

Newcombe was gone, too—

I told him to stay behind, he thought. *I insisted on going alone.*

—but the mummies were still coming. Not actors, but real mummies. The reanimated corpses of the dead. Hundreds of them, shambling toward him, intent on ripping him limb from limb. Their howls of bloodlust reverberated down the passage.

He turned and ran.

I have to get out of here. But how?

The passage stretched out ahead of him, like some kind of infinity mirror in a carnival funhouse. Where was the Door?

How did I get turned around?

He hadn't even taken ten steps since passing through.

"Hurricane!" He shouted. "Doc! Where are you?"

He had left them behind. He still remembered his dire warning. *Beyond that door, reality loses all meaning. We'll get separated, lost in our own nightmares.*

A strange chittering sound filled the air. In the flickering orange glow of the torches lining the walls, he could see them moving, crawling.

Scorpions.

They crunched underfoot as he ran, their gooey bug guts turning the hard stone into a slippery nightmare. If he fell, they would be all over him in an instant, planting their lethal stings. And if they didn't get him, the mummies would.

No, he thought. *There are no mummies. No scorpions. It's all an illusion. Movie magic.*

And if it isn't?

It was. He was certain of it.

He stopped running.

The scorpions were everywhere now, swarming up his legs.

There are no scorpions.

Behind him, the mummies shuffled closer, dragging their undead bodies across the stone with a scraping that reverberated through his bones. Closer.

Every fiber of his being told him to run.

He closed his eyes.

There are no mummies.

He could feel tiny points of pressure against his skin; scorpions, crawling on his hands and arms, on his face.

Dragging. Shuffling. Closer.

"Dodge…"

He opens his eyes and he is… somewhere else.

The sky is the color of dying coals. The earth is gray, like the ashes of a funeral pyre.

Skulls. Everywhere, skulls, staring up at him, accusing him with their empty eyes.

A shadow moves at the edge of his vision, but he refuses to look.

A new illusion, he thinks. A new nightmare.

"No," the shadow says. "And yes."

He knows this voice. He turns, despite himself, and sees an old friend.

"Padre." He shakes his head. "No. This is just another trick."

"And if I tried to convince you otherwise, would you believe me?" The Padre smiles, and that is unusual because Dodge doesn't think he has ever seen the man smile before. "You will have to decide whether what I am telling you is true or just another illusion for you to ignore. What you told Brian was absolutely correct. Reality has no meaning here. Time has no meaning. Nevertheless, time is short. The Prisoner draws near."

"Novotny."

"Novotny is a shell. His mind is gone. Only the Prisoner remains."

"I'll stop him."

"You cannot. If you kill Novotny, he will find another host. The Prisoner is beyond life and death. His spirit is bound to the demon creatures he once summoned into this reality. He believes that he may yet bend them to his will, but it is his will that has been bent to their purposes. His soul will never rest while they are trapped in this world."

"I'll close the Door. I'll close every door. Show me how."

"You misunderstand. This place exists at the threshold. I am the Door that he must open. I am all that stands between your world and…" The Padre gestures to the blighted landscape.

"Molly," Dodge says. "Wittgenstein said she's connected to you. That Novotny will try to attack you through her."

"Yes."

"I'll get her away from him."

"You may. But know that one day, no matter where you go, he will find you. And when he does, you will have but one choice." The Padre falls silent and Dodge understands what is being asked of him.

"No. There has to be another way. Break the link. Close that door."

"Only death can sever the connection."

Only death. Molly's death. *"No. I won't do it."*

"Then night will fall upon your world forever."

As if in response to this dire prophecy, the sky begins to darken. The Padre starts to turn away.

"Wait! I have to try to save her."

"I know," the Padre says in a sad voice as night falls.

"… we have to run!"

A hand grabbed his own, snapping him out of the… dream? Illusion? *That voice,* he thought. *I know that voice.*

A female voice, with a distinctive Irish burr. He looked down and saw close cropped brown hair framing a pixie-like face, eyes magnified by a pair of thick spectacles, looking up at him, imploring him. "Fiona?"

"Come on, Dodge. Hurry." She tugged on his hand, urged him to follow her down the torchlit passage.

Behind them, the darkness was full of horrors. Creatures of smoke and shadow.

Another illusion?

No, he decided. Not completely anyway.

Fiona was real enough. She pulled at his arm, dragging him forward a few steps. "Come. On."

He pulled back, nearly yanking her off her feet. "Fiona, stop it. This isn't real. It's all in your head."

She pointed down the passage at the swirling nightmare. "That's not in my head."

"Yes it is. You passed through the Door of Osiris. Remember?"

"Of course I do. It was just five minutes ago." She pointed again emphatically. "It's a passage to the Realm of Osiris. The Underworld. Hell? Let me know if when I say something that rings a bell."

"It's an illusion," Dodge said, squeezing her hand. "Trust me. Those things can't hurt you."

The smoke monstrosities were close now, close enough that he could feel the hot wind as they pushed the air ahead of them. A foul stench stung his nostrils.

What if Fiona was right?

No. It's not real.

She pulled again, and then when it was apparent that he was not going to follow, she tried to wriggle free. She screamed, a piercing sound that made him want to run, but instead he pulled her close, hugging her tight against his chest as the demons engulfed them and....

"Huh," Fiona said in a somewhat more subdued voice. "I guess you were right."

The only sound now was the insidious hum that had been there all along, lurking beneath the surface of reality. He looked down at Fiona then around at a place he was seeing for the first time.

It was another illusion, had to be. A vast hall, stretching out to infinity but by no means empty. In fact, the room was filled with motionless figures, men wearing unfamiliar garb—a mixture of armor and robes, war helmets and turbans—holding spears and swords. They appeared to be alive, but stood statue still—an army, awaiting the order to attack.

"My goodness," Fiona gasped. "Those are Persian warriors. This is…" She turned to him, her eyes wide with wonder at the significance of this discovery. "This is the lost army of Cambyses. A Persian king sent an army of fifty thousand men to capture the Oracle at the Temple of Amun in Siwa. The entire army, every last man, was consumed by a sandstorm and never seen again. But that was more than two thousand years ago."

"Time has no meaning here, Fiona," Dodge explained. "You've been here for weeks."

"No, that's nonsense."

"Sadiki was forced to leave you here. He…" Dodge stopped himself. There was no telling what effect the shock of learning of her father's death might have on Fiona in this place.

"Why aren't they moving?"

"They're trapped in an illusion. Just like you were when I found you." The explanation felt incomplete. This was an illusion, too. It had to be.

But if that was true, could he trust anything he saw? Anything he felt? Was Fiona real, or just a fiction, created by his subconscious?

He felt something tingling against his palm, and opened his fist to reveal the amulet.

"The djed column," Fiona exclaimed. "Now I remember. I used it to open the…"

She looked away, searching for the door. Dodge looked too and realized that the Persian army of Cambyses had vanished, along with the immense hall. In its place, a small semi-circular chamber, like the other half of the room on the other side of the Door, where his friends were waiting. The room was empty except for them and one other item, a black orb, about the size of a bowling ball, hanging about five feet above the ground, turning slowly like the mirror ball in a dance hall. The surface was studded with spiky protrusions, like rays bursting from the surface of a….

"Black Sun," Dodge whispered.

Fiona glanced up at him. "Interesting. Those are djed columns on the exterior, representing Osiris, the god of the afterlife, and the sun is the symbol of Amun, who ruled above the other gods, but the Egyptians always represented the sun as a disk, not a sphere."

"I think this thing is a lot older than the Egyptians," Dodge said. Without letting go of Fiona, he moved toward the orb, realizing as he did that it wasn't suspended by a wire or chain, but floating in the air in defiance of gravity.

"Those djed columns are exactly the same as my father's amulet," Fiona said.

Dodge winced a little at the mention of Professor Dunn, but her observation was correct. He held up the amulet. "I think this belongs on it."

"What will happen?"

"I don't know," Dodge answered honestly. "Hopefully, we'll get back to the real world."

"Do I need to click my heels together and say 'there's no place like home'?"

Dodge managed a smile. "It might help."

He reached out for the orb. It remained fixed in mid-air, completely unresponsive to his touch, but as it turned he spotted a conspicuous gap in the pattern of djed columns. "That's where our missing piece goes," he said.

As Dodge brought the djed closer, the orb began to glow with purple light. Tendrils of energy, like little lightning bolts, began dancing between the djed columns and then reached out to the artifact in Dodge's hand. He winced as it made contact, but aside from a faint tingling that might have been his imagination, he felt no change.

"There's no place like home," Fiona said again.

He touched the amulet to the surface of the orb.

The humming stopped.

CHAPTER 17— THE PRISONER FREED

The orb dropped to the ground with a thump that shook the ground underfoot. The impact raised a puff of dust that momentarily obscured the relic from view. Dodge jumped back involuntarily, though if any part of him had been under the orb, that part would have been smashed to a pulp.

"Dodge! You did it!" Newcombe exclaimed.

Dodge had not moved, but the world evidently had. The wall which had, physically at least, separated the two chambers was gone. Now, there was just one large circular room. The Osiris Door, the gate to a realm of illusion and madness, the threshold between the dimensions, was not simply closed, but gone completely.

"Findlay!" Fiona broke from Dodge's embrace and rushed into Newcombe's arms. A moment later, she saw the body leaning against the wall and her cry of joy became a wail of grief.

Dodge stood back, allowing Newcombe and Sadiki to comfort the young woman.

"Interesting souvenir you picked up there," Hurricane said in a low voice. "I'm guessing that's what all the fuss is about?"

The dust had settled to reveal the black orb. It had hit the floor with such force that the stone around it had cratered upon impact, but the protruding djed columns were still perfectly straight and undamaged. The object was now completely quiescent; the strange lightshow had ended. The djed amulet had not only affixed itself seamlessly to the sphere, but changed color as well.

"The Black Sun," he said again. He realized that he had been mistaken in thinking that the Osiris Door had vanished. The Black Sun was the Door and the djed amulet was the key that had just locked it up tight.

"Something we can use to fight Novotny and get Molly back?" Hurricane asked.

Molly.

No matter where you go, he will find you. And when he does, you will have but one choice… Only death can sever the connection.

Dodge shook his head. "We have to get rid of it. Throw it in the deepest part of the ocean where Novotny and the Nazis will never find it." He knelt over the object, tentatively touching it. The metal was cold to the touch, cold enough that prolonged contact would probably have caused frostbite, but aside from that, nothing else happened. Dodge stripped off the head-covering he had been wearing, wrapped it around his hands, and tried to lift the orb. It didn't budge.

"Let me give it a go," Hurricane said. He managed to insinuate his fingers under it and growled with the strain. His face grew bright red. The muscles of his arms bulged and then split the seams of his shirt, but the Black Sun did not move even a fraction of a fraction of an inch.

"Here's a thing," Wittgenstein said. "God has created a rock so heavy that even he can't lift it."

Newcombe patted Fiona's shoulder then rose and came to inspect the relic. "Interesting."

"What's it made of, doc?"

"Adamantine I imagine, but adamantine that has become incredibly dense. It has been theorized that stars might collapse under their own weight, compressed by gravity into a material so dense that a teaspoonful of it would weigh more than the entire earth. I doubt we're dealing with something quite so dramatic here, but it is nevertheless quite astonishing."

"It was floating in the air a few minutes ago," Dodge said. "But when it came into contact with the amulet, it suddenly became heavier than lead."

Newcombe gently probed one of the protruding columns. "Curiouser and curiouser. I would surmise that the djed amulets act like attenuators. Similar to magnets in a way. When they are separated, there is an energy potential, and the attraction becomes stronger as the proximity increases, until contact is made and the energy changes state."

"So what you're sayin' is that this thing ain't going anywhere," Hurricane said. "What if we tried pulling off the amulet? Would that reverse the effect?"

"It might," Newcombe said.

"It would also open up Door again," Dodge said. "At least until we got some distance between the djed key and the Black Sun. But it's worth a try." He met Hurricane's gaze. "Better clear everyone out of here."

Newcombe returned to Fiona's side and gently separated her from her father's body. Dodge felt terrible for interfering, but if he couldn't keep the Black Sun out of Novotny's reach, she would never have the opportunity to grieve.

When he was alone, he curled his fingers, still protected by a piece cloth, around one of the djed columns. He could not tell if it was the same one that he had placed on the orb; they were all identical. He felt a little like a knight of yore, trying to draw Excalibur from the stone. Would it work? Would he be found worthy?

The djed amulet came away in his hand, as easy as lifting a salt shaker from a table top. When he opened the cloth covering, he saw that the artifact had regained its silvery appearance.

Almost immediately, the hum returned, growing in intensity with each passing second. The orb began to glow with purple light. Then it began to rise into the air as if feather light. Beneath it, the sand on the floor began to shimmer and organize into circular patterns—Chladni figures, Newcombe had called them—and then they too began to rise, like a curtain dividing the room. The wall was reforming and as Dodge backed away, it seemed to phase back into existence.

The Black Sun was gone, hidden behind the solid barrier.

Dodge shoved the amulet into his pocket and headed back up the passage, but even before he climbed out of the excavation, he could sense that something was wrong.

His friends were all kneeling. Hurricane. Newcombe. Wittgenstein. Fiona....

"Liz?" Her face seemed to glow in the pale moonlight.

"I'm so sorry, Dodge," she whispered

He could see tears glistening on her cheek.

Then he saw the men standing behind them, and the blades held to their throats. They had traded their hawkmen attire for Bedouin robes and curved daggers, but appeared no less lethal. There was no sign of Novotny's dirigible. No doubt the villain had landed the airship some distance away in order make a stealthy approach and take Dodge and his friends by surprise.

Novotny stepped out from behind them. "You have something that I need, Dalton. Give it to me now, and you and your friends may walk away. Refuse or delay, and I will start killing them, one at a time."

Dodge knew it wasn't an empty threat. Any act of resistance would accomplish nothing more than hastening his friends along to their fate, and Novotny would still get what he wanted. But as long as they were alive, there was hope, just a sliver of it but that was better than nothing.

"I won't refuse," he said. "I have the key." He reached slowly into his pocket, drew it out and held it up high. "It's here. Please, just let my friends go. Molly, too. You don't need her." He hadn't see Molly, but he knew she had to be nearby.

You will have but one choice... Only death can sever the connection.

Novonty turned to the man holding Liz. "Kill her."

"No!" Dodge shouted. He threw the djed amulet down on the sand. "Here. Take it. You said you'd let them go."

Novotny raised a hand, staying Liz's execution. He strode forward and picked up the amulet. As he held it up in the moonlight, inspecting it,

Dodge thought he could see a sliver of the man—maybe that was the wrong word—that now wore Novotny's skin.

"You know that they aren't going to let you control them again," Dodge said. "They'll turn on you, use you to destroy everything. You'll die, too. But there's a way to beat them."

Novotny turned to him, a faint glimmer of interest in his eyes. "What do you know of it?"

"I know that you enslaved those…" What had the Padre called them? "Those demons. And I know that they want to make you pay for it. They're using you. Using you to destroy the world and set them free. Don't give into them.

"You already have everything you could possibly want. You have a body. Men who worship you. You even have the key to the Door of Osiris. But if you use Molly to attack the Padre, you will lose everything. You will die."

A strange smile touched Novotny's lips. "I have lived far too long already." He turned again. "Bring her."

One of Novotny's men came forward, bearing a limp form in his arms. *Molly!* Dodge's heart sank. "You bastard."

Yet, he knew that she was still alive. She was the one person Novotny had to keep alive, at least until the Black Sun was within his grasp.

Novotny took Molly in his own arms and began walking toward the excavation. Dodge stepped out of the way, and as he did, he lowered his hands a little. The Luger was still in his belt. It would take him less than a second to draw it, flip the safety catch off, and fire.

But fire at whom?

You will have but one choice… Only death can sever the connection.

No. I won't do that.

Maybe no one had to die.

When Novotny, still clinging to Molly, was just five feet away, Dodge made his move. He leapt forward, drawing the Luger as he did. He didn't fuss with the safety. With any luck, the mere threat of the gun would be enough. In a heartbeat, he was behind Novotny, pressing the pistol to the man's temple.

"Anybody moves, and your boss is a dead man." He jammed the gun barrel against Novotny's head to emphasize his point. "Tell them, Novotny. Tell them to back off."

"Kill me," Novotny said, laughing. "I will come back."

"I don't want to kill you," Dodge said. "I just want you to let my friends go. Let them go, and I'll let you go."

"You're lying."

"I've got no reason to. Let us walk away, and the Black Sun is yours."

Novotny considered this for a moment, then called out a command in Arabic. The men holding his friends exchanged a nervous glance, but then sheathed their blades and moved away.

Hurricane was back on his feet in a flash, both pistols drawn and aimed at the retreating men.

"Brian," Dodge said. "Don't. I meant what I said."

"That monster killed my father," Fiona shouted.

Hurricane shook his head. "Dodge, I know you're a man of word, but just this once, I think you'll be forgiven. We can't let this monster get his hands on that thing."

"Saving Molly is the only thing that matters," Dodge said.

Hurricane frowned but holstered his pistols and moved forward to take Molly from Novotny's arms. "What's wrong with her? What did you do to her?"

Novotny glowered, refusing to answer.

"She'll be okay," Dodge said. "Let's just get her away from here."

"And what's gonna keep him from coming after us?"

"The Black Sun. The Osiris Gate. Whatever you want to call it. It's here and it's not going anywhere."

"And how long do you reckon that'll keep him busy?"

"Long enough for us to get out of here," Dodge said. "Fiona. You're a pilot, right? You think you can fly a dirigible?"

Novotny flinched. "That was not part of our arrangement."

A faint gleam appeared in the young woman's grief swollen eyes. She nodded. "I think I can handle it."

"There you go. It's around here somewhere. Get everyone on board." Dodge relaxed his hold on Novotny, allowing the man to stand on his own, but kept the pistol trained on him. "It's a small price to pay. You can always get a new blimp."

"You must realize that this isn't over, Dalton. I will come for you. Nothing can—" Novotny never finished the sentence. He stiffened, his dead eyes going wide, and then pitched forward like a felled tree.

The sound of a shot echoed across the desert.

Dodge staggered back a step. What the hell?

Novotny was dead. Cut down by a sniper's bullet.

More shots thundered in the air, then Hurricane's shout rose above the din. "Dodge! Get down!"

He dropped to his knees as bullets sizzled through the air above his head. Who's shooting? Novotny's men?

Novotny's men were shooting, but not at Dodge and certainly not at their stricken leader. The shot that had felled Novotny had come from behind them, from somewhere out of the desert, and that was where they were now directing their fire.

Lights flashed in the distance—the headlights of a caravan of approaching vehicles, and the muzzle flashes of machine guns.

"Nazis!"

He could see the convoy clearly now. Kaufmann, his head wrapped in a bandage, was standing in the lead car holding a pistol. Two more vehicles filled with troopers—the survivors of the attack on the compound in Farafra—rolled along behind them, picking off Novotny's men one by one.

They concentrated their fire on any target that fired back, but Dodge knew eventually the Nazis would come looking for the rest of them.

Novotny, the Prisoner's latest host, was dead. The Prisoner's spirit would live on, and eventually find a new body to inhabit, but for the moment at least, the ghost of the ancient sorcerer-scientist was the least of his worries.

"Dodge!" Hurricane shouted again. "Come on!"

The exhortation jolted Dodge into action. The rest of the group had found cover behind the mud-brick walls of the ruin, but Dodge made a grab for Novotny's body, intent on retrieving the djed amulet and denying the Nazis their prize. Before he could move an inch though, the sand around him exploded like a dozen tiny volcanic eruptions. He could feel the heat, the kinetic energy of the heavy caliber rounds, and immediately reversed course before the next volley found him, crawling on all fours toward the relative safety of the ruins.

Kaufmann's vehicle pulled up alongside Novotny's body and the SS commander got out. He stood over the dead man for a moment, savoring his victory, then reached down and began rifling through Novotny's pockets.

"He's going to find the key," Sadiki wailed.

"Fat lot of good it will do him," Fiona muttered. "He'll wind up trapped in there like the army of Cambyses."

Dodge wasn't so sure. If anyone could figure out how to turn the Black Sun—or whatever it really was—into a weapon, it was the Third Reich, but there wasn't a whole lot they could do about it.

"We need to get to Novotny's airship," he said.

"It's moored to some palm trees at the oasis," Liz said. "I can get us there, if the Nazis don't beat us to it."

"We'll cross that bridge when we…" He trailed off as the ground began to vibrate beneath him. "You feel that?"

"An earthquake," Newcombe said.

"Feels more like a battle tank rolling up," Hurricane opined. "But I don't recall seeing one back at Farafra."

The shaking intensified, the desert floor vibrating so fast that Dodge's feet began sinking into it like quicksand.

"It's not a tank," he said. "There's something moving under the sand."

"Something?" Wittgenstein started to ask, but before he could get the question out, a hideous cackling sound silenced him.

Laughter.

The mocking laughter of a triumphant enemy.

An enemy that now wore the skin of the woman Dodge loved.

Kaufmann took the amulet from Novotny's dead hand. He didn't know what it was, but he knew it was something important. Something powerful. Yet he also knew that this was not the Black Sun, not the true object of the Novotny's quest.

What had brought the man here, to this spot in the middle of nowhere? Was the real treasure somewhere close by?

It had been almost a minute since the last shot was fired. The battle was over, the last of Novotny's men, routed. He raised a hand, signaling his troops to rally around him. As he waited for the other vehicles to arrive, he imagined a very different parade, the celebration that awaited him upon his glorious return to the Fatherland. After wresting victory from Himmler's disastrous partnership with the treacherous Novotny, it was not unthinkable that he might be elevated to the position of Reichfuhrer of the Schutzstaffel. At the very least, he would certainly become one of the Fuhrer's inner circle.

A faint tremor shook the ground as the vehicles pulled up beside him, giving a subtle reminder that his victory celebration was premature. He turned to address his men. "Sweep the area. The Black Sun is here, somewhere. The man who finds it will be rewarded."

The troopers, perhaps entertaining their own fantasies of promotions and accolades, gave a hearty cheer and eagerly dismounted their vehicles, but fell silent as another tremor, stronger than the first vibrated up from the desert floor.

Kaufmann frowned. The vehicles, which had all been shut off, could not be the source of the phenomenon.

So what was causing it?

The shaking intensified. The sand began to shift underfoot. The ground was liquefying. The effect was even more pronounced underneath the vehicles, which had already sunk several inches.

The cheer turned into a murmur of fear. Kaufmann shared their apprehension, and while he was not about to show cowardice in front of his men, there was something to be said for the wisdom of a discretionary retreat. "Move the vehicles away from here. Quickly!"

Three engines immediately roared to life, but before any of the cars could move, the ground gave a lurch that knocked Kaufmann off his feet.

Something flashed in the moonlight. It looked to Kaufmann like a thick rivulet of water…no, molten metal, mercury perhaps, erupting from the sand. It rose into the air alongside the nearest car then fell over it, wrapping completely around the vehicle, a quicksilver python coiling around its prey.

The driver screamed and then was silenced as the coil engulfed him as well, then there was an earsplitting shriek of tortured metal as the entire car folded at the middle. Kaufmann scrambled away frantically as the car was pulled down into the sand, swallowed whole.

"Go!" He screamed.

The two remaining cars tore away in different directions, the dismounted troopers desperately running after them. Kaufmann ran as well.

There was another truncated scream and Kaufmann caught a flash of movement in the corner of his eye. He glanced sideways as an MP-38 fell to the sand. There was no sign of the man who had held the weapon a moment before.

Another silvery tentacle seized the vehicle Kaufmann was following, raising it into the air as effortlessly as a child playing with a toy carved out of wood, and then just as easily smashed it down. There was an eruption of sand, and then a fraction of a second later, a fiery flash as something—

either the fuel tanks or some piece of military ordnance—detonated. The flames glinted off the metallic monstrosity, giving it the appearance of a column of divine fire, towering above the desert floor.

A shot rang out. Then another and then the air was filled with the reports of machine pistols. His surviving men, seeing the futility of trying to flee, had abandoned the last remaining car and were firing at the...whatever it was, giving him an opportunity to escape.

He vowed that their sacrifice would not be in vain.

The fiery column whipped down and began undulating across the sand like an enormous serpent, driving straight for the troopers. Kaufmann turned away, focusing on the dark desert ahead of him, running as fast as his legs would carry him. Behind him, the shooting diminished as, one by one, his men were obliterated. He heard one last burst from an MP-38, then the only sound was of his own boots crunching on the sand.

He stopped. Maybe the creature—he didn't know what else to call it— was drawn to sound. He froze completely, trying to quiet his frantic breathing. His heart was pounding in his chest... could the monstrosity hear that, too?

As he stood there, he could feel the vibrations of the thing moving through the sand, growing more intense as it closed on him.

It knows where I am.

He broke into a run again, but only got a few steps before something snagged his booted foot and lifted him off the ground. He screamed and struggled, but his efforts were futile. The silvery tendril snaked around his leg, slithered up it like a corkscrew to encircle his body and his right arm. He tried to pull free but the tentacle was as hard and unyielding as iron. After a moment, he sagged in its grip, too exhausted to continue the fight and surrendered himself to his fate. It would be a painful death, he had no doubt about that, but he prayed it would be quick.

But the creature did not kill him. There was an insistent pressure against his forearm then the limb was bent at the elbow. The metal coil was manipulating his arm like he was some kind of living marionette. His hand was forcibly thrust into the pocket of his jacket, the pocket where he had stashed the relic from Novotny's body. He felt it brush against his fingers, then his hand involuntarily closed over it.

The creature spun him around until he was facing the old ruins, then it, along with him as an unwilling passenger, began moving in that direction. For the first time since the attack began, it occurred to him that the creature was made of the same metal as Novotny's artifact.

Despair closed over Dodge's heart like a fist.

"Molly."

Hurricane echoed his groan, then the big man drew one of his pistols and aimed it at the laughing woman.

"No," Dodge said, putting himself between them. "Hurricane, you can't."

The big man's face was grim, grimmer than Dodge had ever seen. "It's not her anymore, Dodge."

"She's still in there. She can fight him. Just like Captain Falcon did."

"Maybe so. But Cap couldn't kick him out."

Captain Falcon, Hurricane's old commanding officer and the Prisoner's first host, had waged a quiet war against his disembodied possessor, subtly goading the villain into seeking out his old comrades. In the end, he had broken the Prisoner's hold just long enough to take his own life, banishing the wandering spirit, if only for a little while.

"We have to try," Dodge pleaded.

Molly stopped laughing, her expression twisting into a mask of alarm. "Don't shoot."

He could hear the deception in the voice. It wasn't Molly speaking, pleading for her life, but the Prisoner, stalling for time.

"Molly would rather die than have you wearing her skin like an old coat," Hurricane growled. "Dodge, you know what we have to do. Look at what's happening out there? One of those pillar thingamajigs slipped the Padre's leash."

Dodge had already figured that much out. At least one of the other-dimensional entities, though still trapped inside a shell of adamantine, had broken loose from the grappling match with Father Nathan Hobbs and traveled the distance from Udaygiri Cave to Egypt with impossible swiftness. This was the very thing the Padre had warned him about. The Prisoner was using the psychic bond Molly shared with her adopted father to attack or distract the Padre, freeing the entities to pass through Osiris Door as soon as it was opened.

"We have to do this," Hurricane said. "Before it's too late."

"That thing has Kaufmann," Newcombe called out. "It's bringing him this way. We need to go."

"Dodge, listen to me." Hurricane's voice was uncharacteristically solemn. "Get everyone else to safety. I can handle this. You shouldn't be here."

Dodge felt as if his heart was being torn in two. He knew Hurricane was right, but part of him refused to accept it. He turned, looking Molly in the eye, searching for some trace of her, any indication that she was still there, fighting to be free of the Prisoner.

Her pleading face, a mockery of the real Molly, twisted into a look of real horror. Her hand shot out and seized his. "You know what has to be done" Her voice was a hoarse whisper. "Only death can break the connection."

Only death....

It wasn't Molly, but it wasn't the Prisoner either. "Padre?"

Molly spoke again, but the words were not hers. "I'm here. He's fighting me. You have to break the connection now, before the Door is opened. Before he can set them free. You have to do it, Dodge. There is no other way."

"Dodge!" Liz shouted. "It just took Kaufmann underground. I think we're out of time here."

"Go!" Hurricane urged.

You will have but one choice. Only death....

"You're right," Dodge said. "We have to kill Molly. It's the only way."

Just saying it was enough to bring tears to Dodge's eyes.

Hurricane nodded and leveled the pistol at her. Molly—or whomever was truly controlling her—nodded and closed her eyes.

"No Hurricane," Dodge said again, his voice steadier. "Don't shoot her. There's another way."

"If we stop her heart, the Prisoner will be forced out of her body," Dodge said. *And the connection to the Padre will be broken,* he thought but didn't say aloud. "Then we can bring her back."

Hurricane blinked at him. "Bring her back?"

"It can be done. An electrical shock can restart a stopped heart." He looked to Newcombe for support and expert advice. Molly was the real medical expert, but if anyone else could confirm his idea, it was Newcombe. "That's true, isn't it? Just like Dr. Frankenstein?"

The scientist nodded slowly. "There is a method for electrical defibrillation, but Dodge... It requires placing electrodes directly on the heart muscle. We would have to open up her chest cavity. And then there would still be the problem of generating an electrical current."

Dodge felt the slim thread of hope slipping through his fingers, but then Wittgenstein pointed out across the desert. A hundred or so yards away, sat an abandoned Nazi military vehicle. "That thing has a battery and an alternator. There's your current."

"Is it possible to shock someone's heart without surgery?" Dodge pressed.

"Well, of course," Newcombe admitted. "It's called electrocution and it's often fatal. Of course, I have no idea if an automobile's electrical system can generate sufficient amperage to do much of anything.

"If she's already dead, it can't make things worse."

Newcombe still looked uncertain, but Hurricane made the decision. "Get going Doc. Figure out how make it work."

Newcombe looked over at Wittgenstein. "I could use an extra pair of hands?"

"I'm afraid that's about all I'll be good for."

"I can help," Fiona put in.

"Go!" Dodge shouted.

As the rest of the group headed for the derelict vehicle, Hurricane swept Molly up in his arms again. "I think I know how to kill her without really killing her," he said, "But I don't know if it's gonna be enough to fool her hitchhiker."

Dodge nodded. "We have to try."

Ahead of them, Newcombe and Fiona had the hood cover open and were already tinkering with the engine while the others looked on. Liz glanced up and saw Hurricane and Dodge coming, then she pointed to something behind them. Dodge looked back and saw something emerge from the old ruins.

It resembled nothing less than the writhing head of Medusa. Not one, but at least a dozen of the extradimensional entities wriggled out of the excavation, their shells of molten adamantine intertwined and squirming like a nest of snakes. Although partly hidden by the squirming extrusions of liquid metal, Dodge could see that the entities were carrying the Black Sun.

But how is that possible?

He surmised that the entity had used Kaufmann as a proxy to reveal the orb and placing the amulet on it in order to bring it fully into the real world. In so doing, they had opened the way to what the Padre had called the Threshold—a shortcut to the same other-dimensional space where the Padre stood watch, blocking the escape route of the pillar entities. Yet, activating the Black Sun ought to have made the orb impossibly heavy.

Too heavy for a human at least.

The extradimensional entities had proven very adept at manipulating adamantine. No doubt whatever gave the Black Sun its otherworldly powers derived from a similar source, so lifting and moving the otherworldly object would have posed no difficulty for them.

Whatever the explanation, the entity controlling Kaufmann had summoned reinforcements. More entities, perhaps all of them, had broken free of the unending struggle with the Padre and emerged back into the real world using the Black Sun itself.

Now all that remained was for the Prisoner to use the Black Sun one last time to set them free.

"Hurricane. We're out of time." Dodge had to force the words past the lump in his throat. "Do it now."

Hurricane dropped to his knees on the sand, and with deliberate swiftness, placed one of his massive hands over Molly's mouth and nose. Molly's eyes went wide and she immediately began struggling.

"Hold her, Dodge."

Dodge gripped Molly's arms then threw himself over her, hugging her tight. He could feel her the spasms in her chest as she fought in vain to draw a breath, could hear the runaway staccato of her heartbeat, escalating with primal fear and desperation. He tried to tell himself that it was the Prisoner, and not Molly, but he couldn't make himself believe it, and it probably didn't matter anyway. Molly was convulsing in his arms, fighting tooth and nail to live.

Dodge wondered what would happen when her brain, starved of oxygen, finally shut down. Would she just fall asleep?

Would they be able to wake her up?

He turned his head, unable to bear watching any longer, and saw the writhing mass of living adamantine moving relentless forward. They knew what he and Hurricane were doing, knew that when Molly died, her link to their jailor would be severed and their chances of escaping the universe of man would die as well.

They were not about to let that happen.

A silver tentacle snaked out from the tangle and lashed at Dodge. Every fiber of his being told him to let go of Molly and throw himself out of the way, but he squeezed tighter. The tendril slapped the sand, mere inches from him, then rose up and arched over him like the head of a cobra.

"It's just tryin' to scare us" Hurricane said through clenched teeth. "Don't pay it no mind."

Dodge was certainly scared, but his real fear was that the entities might escalate their attempt to drive him and Hurrricane away from Molly. The squirming mass moved closer, and more tendrils reached out to menace them. Long snakes of liquid adamantine began probing him, encircling him, testing his defenses.

He had seen how destructive they could be, but they were also capable of delicate precision, as when they had plucked Kaufmann up, entwining him and turning him into a living marionette. They could do the same to him. Maybe the only reason they hadn't was because they were afraid of what might happen to Molly in the process, but as Hurricane brought the young woman closer to death's door, the entities would almost certainly take off the gloves.

"Hurricane," he rasped. "Whatever happens, don't stop."

"What?"

Dodge let go of Molly and then launched himself straight up into the writhing mass. The adamantine bodies might have looked like long extrusions of quicksilver, but they were as hard and unyielding as the suspension cables on the Brooklyn Bridge. He grasped hold of them, pulling himself deeper into their midst, and then he found what he was looking for.

The Black Sun.

He closed his fist over one of the djed columns and pulled…

Dodge lay on a floor of stone, surrounded by figures wearing hooded robes. Their garments reminded him of the attire worn by monks, but underneath were monstrous bodies—tall, but twisted like ancient stone gargoyles crouching on the battlements of a medieval fortress. They reached out for him with appendages that were more claws than hands. He shrank back, looking for a way out of the circle. They followed him with eyes that glowed like coals, but their movements were slow, as if they were trying to move through molasses.

The Padre is slowing them down.

Without the Padre's intervention, he probably would not have been able to reach the Black Sun and remove one of the attenuating djed columns.

He spotted the orb itself, hanging in the air above him at the center of the circle of entities. The amulet was still clenched in his fist, humming, vibrating.

The noise of a struggle reached him. He evaded the groping hand of the entities and slipped past them. He was in a circular chamber, identical to the hidden room under the ruins, but he knew that this place was nowhere on earth.

Molly and the Padre were fighting, grappling with each other like Jacob and the angel.

Molly saw him first. "Dodge. Help me."

"Don't listen to it," the Padre said. "You know it's not her."

Do I? Dodge wondered.

"He's using her to destroy me," the Padre said. He was breathless from the exertion, and Dodge found that unusual. The Padre was a master of unarmed combat. "The link between us. Only death can break it."

Only death. Molly's death.

"Don't let him kill me," Molly pleaded, but Dodge couldn't tell if it was Molly or the Prisoner.

Did it even matter?

The Prisoner was using Molly's psychic bond to attack Father Hobbs, weakening his defenses against the other-worldly entities. If the Padre fell in that battle, the world would end. If Molly died and the link was severed, the Prisoner would survive, cast out to wander the earth in search of another host, but he would never again have the ability to strike directly at the Padre. His evil would endure, but so would the world.

Sacrifice one life to save the world. It was a simple calculation, and yet Dodge hesitated. Was it weakness? Were his feelings for Molly blinding him to the harsh reality of the situation?

I'm missing something, he thought.

"Dodge!" The Padre shouted. "You have to do this now. We're running out of time."

Time.

That's it.

Reality has no meaning here. The Padre had told him that. Time has no meaning.

Whatever it is I think I'm seeing, Dodge realized, *it's not real. It can't be trusted. It's an illusion, but whose illusion?*

"Molly," he whispered.

He leapt forward into the fray, shoving Molly away and wrapping his arms around the Padre…except it wasn't Father Nathan Hobbs now, but someone else.

Something else.

A thing made of smoke and shadows, and yet somehow, he held onto it.

Molly fell to her knees, as if losing contact with her assailant had stolen her vital energy. Her hands came up to her mouth and she shuddered, gasping for a breath that would not come.

A voice hissed from the dark thing in Dodge's grasp. "Release me! Or your world will burn."

But Dodge did not let go. The threat was a desperate attempt at deception, as hollow and empty as the creature that uttered it.

The creature into whose illusion he had trespassed.

The struggle he had witnessed had not been the Padre, fighting the Prisoner in Molly's body for control of the entities, but rather Molly herself fighting the prisoner for control of her own body.

Now, she was free of him.

Dodge wrestled the Prisoner back toward the ring of entities, shrugging off their attempts to seize him. The amulet began to tingle in his clenched fist, radiating violet energy. Above him, the Black Sun came alive, throwing out streams of purple energy like lightning bolts.

Then, he thrust the amulet against the Black Sun, and....

...tumbled forward onto the sand.

The Black Sun was gone, and so were the entities which had been holding it.

How...?

He wasn't sure it was even the right question.

He looked down and saw that the djed amulet was still clenched in his fist.

"What just happened?" a familiar voice—Liz—exclaimed behind him.

He whirled around and saw Hurricane, still holding Molly's motionless form, still smothering her with his massive hand. "Let go of her," he shouted, suddenly in a panic.

"Dodge..."

With strength born of both fear and anger, Dodge tore the big man's hand away from Molly's face. "He's gone," he shouted as he pulled her away. "The Prisoner is gone. We have to bring to bring her back."

Hurricane's eyes went wide in a look of horror, but he immediately let go of Molly, releasing her into Dodge's embrace. "Doc, we need that electric shock pronto."

"It's not ready," Newcombe cried out.

Dodge ignored them. He laid Molly on her back and pressed his face to hers. Nothing.

He felt something heavy against his shoulder, a hand—Hurricane's— gently pulling him back. "Dodge. I'm sorry."

"No," he shouted back. "She's alive. I know she's alive."

He shrugged off the hand and threw his arms around her, squeezing her tight, as if by doing so, he might keep her soul from escaping her body.

"I know you're still in there, Moll. You didn't give in to him. Don't give in to this."

"I'm sorry," Hurricane said again, his voice a solemn rumble like distant thunder. "There was no other way. We knew this might happen."

Dodge barely heard him, He pressed his face against Molly's cheek, feeling the smear of hot tears between them. "Don't leave me," he whispered. "I love you."

Molly flinched in his arms and then her eyes opened wide, arms flailing as if waking from a nightmare of falling. She drew in a ragged breath which turned into a coughing fit.

Hurricane grasped hold of Dodge again, but this time there was no gentleness as he pulled Dodge away. "Give her some space," he roared.

The others rushed forward, surrounding Molly as she fought to get her breathing under control. Dodge just sat back on the ground, both exhausted and relieved beyond all measure.

Molly was still alive, and for a few seconds at least, that was the only thing that mattered.

After a few moments, Wittgenstien cleared his throat. "At the risk of raining on anyone's parade, how can we be sure she's really herself again?"

"She is," Dodge said, quickly. "The Prisoner is gone. Trapped on the other side of the Osiris Door."

Molly raised her eyes, nodded and croaked, "I'll even let you hypnotize me again to prove it."

Wittgenstein conceded the point, but then turned to Dodge. "Isn't that where he wanted to be?"

Dodge shook his head. "He's stuck there. A Prisoner again, as long as no one opens the Door."

He didn't explain how he knew this. He wasn't sure he actually did know, but it felt like the right answer.

The Prisoner's plan had been to use the psychic link between Molly and the Padre to insinuate his consciousness into the latter, whereupon he would regain complete control over the entities he had once enslaved. Once dispossessed from Molly, that avenue of attack was gone, and without access to another host body, there was no way for him to cross back into the physical universe.

He stared down at the amulet. The Black Sun had slipped back into the Realm of Osiris, the Threshold space between dimensions, but as long as there was a key to unlock that door, the possibility of another escape by the Prisoner could not be completely dismissed. "We need to get rid of this. Take it somewhere where it won't ever be found."

Kaufmann pulled himself forward with his one good arm, clawing his way from the chamber where the monstrosity had left him, discarded him like a disposable paper cup, after using him to retrieve the Black Sun from behind some kind of hidden door.

Both the creature and the Black Sun were gone, but that momentary glimpse of the artifact had filled him with hope, and that hope was what now kept him going despite his injuries.

Every inch of progress was an excruciating ordeal. The creature had broken one of his arms, broken or sprained an ankle, cracked several ribs, but he did not allow himself the luxury of misery. The Black Sun was real. It was powerful beyond all his expectations. It had been within his grasp, and he vowed that it would be again.

He dragged himself down the narrow passage to the excavation trench, heaved himself up onto the sand and, despite the debilitating waves of agony that radiated from his broken bones, managed to prop himself up against the broke wall of the ruin.

All was still. There was no sign of his men, nor of the creature that had destroyed them. It was as if the desert had swallowed them whole. Erased them from existence.

But what was that strange humming sound?

He turned his head this way and that, trying to pinpoint the source. It seemed to be everywhere, growing louder.

It sounded like it was right on top of him.

He looked up and saw it, an enormous silhouette, like the hull of a massive warship, sailing through the sky above him.

Novotny's airship.

Novotny was dead, he was certain of that, but perhaps someone had survived…. "Dalton!" He spat the name like a curse.

Novotny had been right to fear Dodge Dalton. The American was as resilient as a cockroach. There was not a doubt in his mind that Dalton had not only captured the airship but also the Black Sun.

Capturing it and keeping it however were two very different things. The desert was vast and Kaufmann had the military resources of the Third Reich at his disposal.

"Fly away, Dalton," he whispered. "But I will find you. I will blast you from the skies and take the Black Sun from your dead hands."

The sun was just breaking in the east as the Mediterranean Sea came into view ahead of them. After a night of being shot at, beat up, and blown up, by Nazis, madmen and extra-dimensional entities, the airship journey was a welcome respite.

Novotny's dirigible, while nowhere near as extravagant as the Majestic, the enormous zeppelin built by renegade industrialist Walter Barron, which according to some accounts had been destroyed by Dodge Dalton in a fiery explosion over New York City, was nevertheless well-appointed with creature comforts necessary for long-distance travel. There was a fully stocked pantry, a bunkroom—presumably for quartering the hawkmen—and a master suite with s soft bed and a small wine collection. There was also an armory and equipment storage room, with rifles, machine guns, small artillery pieces, and more than a dozen sets of adamantine wings.

The latter was of little interest to the weary group that boarded the dirigible at Ain Della. Food, rest and first aid were priorities, as was figuring out how to pilot the craft. Despite, or perhaps because of her recent loss, Fiona threw herself into the task. Although Dodge and Molly were both experienced airplane pilots, Fiona—who had worked with Walter Barron before his diabolical intentions were revealed—had some actual experience with lighter-than-air aircraft, and as she familiarized herself with the controls, she was able to put her grief aside. While the others rested and feasted in the airship's salon, Dodge sat with her, shadowing her and learning the ropes, and when he felt comfortable soloing, spelled her so she could get a meal, her first in a very long time.

They traveled on a northeasterly heading until reaching the Nile, and then followed the river north toward Cairo and the Nile Delta. They had been over the expansive verdant triangle for nearly an hour, and now the goal was finally within reach.

There was no discussion about what had happened, what they had endured. There would be plenty of time for that later, and until the djed key was safely at the bottom of the Mediterranean, guaranteeing that the Prisoner would never again be free to torment them, any celebration would have been premature. With the goal now in sight, Dodge dared to allow himself to believe that it was almost over.

"Guys!" Hurricane's shout reverberated through the gondola like a bell. "We've got company."

Dodge peered out the window, scanning the skies for the source of his friend's apprehension, and spotted a single dark speck racing toward them from the west. His first thought was that it was a hawkman, one of Novotny's men who had escaped the Nazi attack, but of course even if that were true, the wings were useful only for non-powered flight—gliding—and there was no way a hawkman could have kept up with motorized dirigible, much less remained aloft for the hours it had taken them to cross the desert.

There was a simpler explanation for what he was seeing, but what it portended was harder to divine. It was an airplane, small and very fast judging by the speed with which it drew close, and on a direct intercept course.

Hurricane burst into the control room and pressed his face to the window even as the aircraft banked and veered past the nose of the airship, passing so close that Dodge could see the distinctive camouflage pattern— back spots against desert tan, like a leopard—and a distinctive straight-armed black cross on each wing—the balkenkreuz, the insignia of the German Wehrmacht.

"That's an Me-109," Fiona said. "A fighter plane."

"Kaufmann must have gotten the word out," Dodge surmised.

"It shouldn't be here. This is Egyptian territory, and Egypt has a treaty with Britain. They can't just fly about willy-nilly."

"The Nazis have a bad habit of doing what they please wherever they please," Hurricane muttered.

The plane executed a tight turn and came around for another pass, waggling its wings back and forth as it cut in front of them again.

"I think they're telling us to put down," Fiona said.

"Can we make it to Port Said?" Dodge asked.

"Maybe," she said. "I guess it depends on our friend out there. Something tells me he won't be as polite on the next pass."

"I know," Dodge said, rising from his seat. "And we're going to answer him in kind."

"Now you're talking," Hurricane said with a grin.

"We won't survive a fire-fight," Fiona warned. "All it will take is one tracer round to ignite the hydrogen and we're cooked."

"If they wanted us dead, they would have done that already. They want us alive. Or they want something they think we have."

"That'll keep us alive a little while," Hurricane said. "But I'd just as soon not end up recreating the Hindenburg."

"A little while is all we need. Port Said is under British control. They have troops there. The Nazis won't dare follow us there."

"When all this is over," Hurricane muttered, "you and me are gonna have a talk about what Nazis will dare to do."

Dodge returned a tight grin. He knew his statement was mostly wishful thinking. If Kaufmann believed they possessed the Black Sun or the means to deliver it, he would not hesitate to start a war with Britain, something his boss the Fuhrer was probably already planning to do anyway.

As he moved through the salon, he warned the others to be ready for an attack. "Move away from the windows," he warned the others.

"That might not make much difference," Hurricane said quietly as they continued into the armory. "That Messerschmitt's cannons will go clean through this gondola."

"I know," Dodge said, walking past the gun racks.

Hurricane saw where he was going. "Oh, no. Not those."

Dodge grabbed one of the folded wing apparatuses and held it out to the big man. "Come on, haven't you ever dreamed of flying like a bird?"

"Nope. I tolerate airplanes and these gas bags, but I'm happiest with both feet firmly on the ground. And I've just about had my fill of those gadgets."

"Don't worry," Dodge said with a laugh. "We aren't going to be using these to fly. They're made of adamantine. We can use them as shields."

Hurricane inclined his head. "Okay, that might work."

Liz poked her head into the room. "That plane just shot at us."

"At us, or was it a warning shot?"

"How am I supposed to know the difference?"

'Did he hit us?"

"No."

"Warning shot." Dodge and Hurricane said it simultaneously.

Dodge passed another of the wing sets to Liz, who held it at arm's length with an incredulous look on her face until Dodge explained what to do with it. In short order, they created a shield wall of wings around the passengers, while Hurricane unlimbered a long-barreled MG-34 machine gun, draping several belts of linked ammunition across his shoulders. Dodge glanced out the window and saw the fighter plane coming around again, lining up for a broadside attack.

"This is it," he shouted. He ran ahead the control room, spreading another set of wings out to shelter himself and Fiona as the cannons on the Me-109 began flashing.

There was a shrieking, splintering sound, like trees snapping apart in a tornado, as bullets tore through the gondola. Dodge could feel the impacts vibrating through the cabin, and then something struck the wings and nearly knocked him down.

A moment later, a different sound filled the interior of the gondola, the harsh buzzsaw of Hurricane returning fire through an open window. Dodge poked his head above the top of his impromptu shield and saw a fist-sized hole in the bulkhead where the German pilot's bullet had hit—and promptly bounced off the indestructible adamantine. He also saw the fighter plane peeling off after its strafing run.

There was a puff of smoke as at least one of Hurricane's bullets found its mark, and the Messerschmitt began trailing a long finger of black smoke across the sky.

Behind them, Hurricane let out a whoop of triumph.

Dodge left the wings where they were and headed back to check on the others. Although the side of the gondola was riddled with holes and most of the windows had been shattered, allowing the wind to rush in, the wings had kept everyone safe.

Hurricane looked back from behind his makeshift shielded gun emplacement. "Gave him a bloody nose. He won't be back."

"Maybe not, but he might have friends. We may need to think about jumping ship."

"Jumping?" Hurricane's brow furrowed. "You mean that literally, don't you?"

"Like Fiona said, we're on a flying bomb here. Now that they know we'll fight back, the gloves are going to come off. One bullet…one spark, and we go up in smoke."

"I didn't see any parachutes…" Hurricane frowned. "You're not thinking… you said we wouldn't be flying with those things."

Dodge grinned but shook his head. "No wings, and no parachutes. If we can make it to the canal, we'll come in low and take a high dive."

Hurricane stroked his chin thoughtfully. "Not bad. The only mighty big 'if' is whether we can reach the canal." His gaze came back to Dodge. "And then there's the wrinkle of what to do with that amulet."

"I'd rather the British get it than the Nazis, but one problem at a time, right?"

"Keep your eyes on the skies." He turned back to the rest of the group. "Listen up. We're going to abandon ship over water. We'll come in low. All you have to do is yell 'cannonball' and take the plunge."

They all stared back at him for a moment, so he added, "Everyone knows how to swim, right?"

"Three more fighters incoming," Hurricane called out.

Dodge rushed to the big man's side and spotted the planes, three specks in the distance, but unquestionably heading right for the airship. "Make sure everyone stays down."

He ran ahead to warn Fiona, but when he got to the control room, she pointed straight ahead. "There it is. Port Said. The Suez Canal. We made it."

"Not quite. We've got three more fighters headed our way. Is there any way to make this sack of gas go faster?"

Fiona answered by pushing the engine throttles fully ahead. The sudden acceleration almost caused Dodge to topple over backward. "We won't be able to keep this up for too long," Fiona warned.

"All we need is a couple more minutes." He looked at the side window, tracking the three planes which were now close enough for him to definitely identify as German Me-109s.

There was an orange flash from the lead aircraft.

"Incoming!" Dodge ducked behind the wings a fraction of a second before the burst raked the gondola. With three planes, he expected the attack to be that much fiercer, but to his amazement, the fire ceased as quickly as it had begun.

Liz burst into the control room, panting to catch her breath. "Hurricane says they're breaking off. Did we make it?"

Dodge looked forward and saw the quarter-mile wide ribbon of the Suez Canal, directly ahead. Evidently, the German pilots were not ready to commit an act of open aggression over British held territory. "I think we did. Go tell everyone to get ready to jump."

"Jump?" Fiona asked. "Shouldn't we just put down?"

Dodge shook his head but didn't explain. "I've got this. Head on back. When I give a shout, start jumping."

Without waiting for her reply, he angled the elevators, so that the flow of air pushed the aircraft down despite the lighter than air gas in the envelope above. The buoyant aircraft shuddered, fighting against the maneuver, against him. Venting off some of the hydrogen would have been a more effective way to descend, but he didn't know nearly enough about operating the dirigible to risk it. Bleeding out too much gas would send the airship crashing down, probably killing them all. Besides, he was going to need lift for what he had planned next.

The three fighter planes were keeping their distance, flying figure-eights like moths flitting about outside a brightly lit window. Dodge wondered if they were in radio contact with their superiors, Kaufmann even, asking whether or not to take the pursuit into territory occupied by the British. If Kaufmann was in control, they almost certainly would, no matter the consequences.

The nose of the dirigible was a hundred feet up, the gondola almost clipping some of the taller roof-tops near the edge of the canal. Then they were over the water.

He eased the throttles back a little—he would also need functioning engines—and steered north, following the course of the canal. The dirigible started to rise almost right away, forcing him to throttle up again.

He shouted over his shoulder. "Jump now!"

There was no way to know if they were complying, though he thought he heard the occasional shout of joy… or terror. Then Hurricane shouted, "Dodge. You coming?"

"Go!" he shouted, "I'll be right there."

He waited five seconds. Ten. "Hurricane, if you're still here, give me a shout!"

No answer. "Good enough."

He eased off the throttle again and flattened out the elevators, allowing the dirigible to drift up. Port Said and the gateway to the Mediterranean Sea lay just ahead, a minute away at his current speed, maybe less. Beyond that, the sea, where he would consign the djed amulet to the depths.

Someone dropped into the co-pilot's chair beside him. "Changed your mind about going for a swim?"

"Molly?" For a few seconds, he could only stare at her in consternation. "You were supposed to jump."

"So were you. But I figured you had another plan." There was a bitterness in her voice that surprised him. "Make sure everyone else gets out then make a noble sacrifice to save the world, right?"

"Is there something wrong with that?"

"Nothing. I'm used to. My dad did it. Captain Falcon did it. Why shouldn't you?"

"It's not like that, Moll."

"Isn't it?" She pointed the window. "You're going to fly out there and drop the amulet into the sea, right? How far do you think the Nazis are going to let you get?"

"Far enough. Molly, you have to trust me. I've got a plan. This isn't a suicide mission."

"Fine. Then you won't mind having me tag along."

The point was moot. They were already beyond the point of no return, but Dodge wasn't about to concede the argument. "I didn't go through Hell to save you just so you could risk your life like this."

"No, you didn't," she shot back, her voice rising with something that wasn't quite anger. "You brought me back, Dodge. You saved me from him. How could you think I would ever let you go it alone after that?"

"I don't need saving, Molly." There was nothing but open water ahead of and below now, but the dirigible was far too close to shore, the water too shallow, for him to be certain of losing the djed amulet for good. Outside the window, the Me-109s continued to loop back and forth at the edge of some undefined boundary.

"I told you," he continued. "I've got a plan. I'm going to get this thing out over open water, and then I'm going to use the wings to fly back to land."

She nodded as if this was what she expected him to say. "You figured out how to use them?"

"I think so. I watched Novotny's men using them. It's a little like swimming. I'll figure the rest out on the way down."

"I guess we will," she said with a defiant grin. "But that's not what I meant. I'm not here to save you. I'm here to save the world with you."

"I don't need—"

"It's not about what you need or don't need. There's nowhere I would rather be than at your side, right here, right now."

Dodge shook his head in disbelief. "The Adventures of Dodge and Molly," he muttered.

"What's that?"

"Nothing. Something Liz was trying to tell me."

"She's a smart lady. You should listen to her. I did."

Dodge glanced over at her.

"She says you're still in love with me."

"That's not exactly a big scoop," Dodge remarked.

"I told her sometimes that's not enough. But I was wrong. It's everything. It's all that matters."

Dodge took a deep breath, let it out with a sigh, and then held out his hand. "All right, then. Let's save the world together."

She took his hand, gave it a squeeze. "I hope you're right about those wings." She pointed past him, out the window. "Here they come."

Dodge didn't know if the airship had passed beyond that invisible boundary defining the Suez Canal protection zone, or if the German pilots had been given the go-ahead to press their attack, but either way, the three fighter planes had broken out of their holding pattern and were moving in a staggered formation toward the dirigible.

Dodge adjusted the elevator controls for added lift, and as the deck beneath him began to tilt up, he pulled Molly down behind the wings.

A thunderous shudder rippled through the gondola as the barrage of lead hammered into it. Dodge felt the wings shaking under sledge-hammer-like impacts. The bulkheads splintered under the combined assault and a blast of wind rushed through the cabin as huge pieces of it broke away. The damage was not merely cosmetic however. Even after the volley ceased, the shuddering continued, like a car with a flat tire scraping along the road.

"I think we just lost an—"

The loud whump of a distant explosion cut him off.

"That's not good," Molly said, even as the temperature around them flashed furnace hot.

"Nope. We're on fire. Time to go." Dodge folded the wings, careful to avoid the razor sharp feather tips. He then turned to open the door leading back to the salon....

Except there was no salon. Beyond the door, the gondola had been reduced to disconnected pieces, with gaping holes in the bulkheads and decks. Everything that wasn't bolted down to what remained of the passenger compartment had already fallen away into the sea hundreds of feet below. That included all the spare wing sets. Worse, through the holes, Dodge could see a blossoming cloud of fire as the hydrogen in the envelope ignited.

Suddenly, Dodge felt fifty pounds lighter. The airship was falling out of the sky.

He buckled on the wings and then wrapped Molly's arms around his waist. "Hold on tight."

Her eyes went wide, but she withheld protest, pressing her head against his chest and squeezing so hard, Dodge could barely breathe.

"Wait," he gasped. He took out the amulet. "Take this. Once we're clear, get rid of it."

She nodded in understanding, loosening her grasp long enough to take it from him. Then, she raised her head up and kissed him.

It was a quick peck, a promise of more to come.

As if he needed one more reason to survive.

He stepped through the door and surrendered himself to gravity.

They fell much faster than the doomed dirigible, and as soon as Dodge was certain that they were clear, he gripped the control handles and spread his arms out, unfurling the adamantine wings. The wings caught the air like a broken kite, flipping Dodge over and throwing him into an out of control tumble.

"Hang on!" he shouted, unnecessarily since Molly's grip seemed even tighter now.

Swimming, he told himself, twisting the control handles and trying different arm positions in an attempt to get control. Nothing seemed to work, and as he turned crazily, he saw, in flashes, the sea rushing up below and the flaming airship above.

This isn't working, he thought, starting to panic.

"Fly!" Molly shouted. She might have said more in explanation; he could barely hear her through the rush of wind from the free fall. Nevertheless, that one word was enough.

Fly.

He had wings. Like an eagle. Like an airplane.

Don't swim. Fly.

A line from an old poem flashed through his head.

In skating over thin ice, our safety is in our speed.

Flying required speed, going so fast that air moving across the airfoil shape of the wings created lift. It was as true for eagles as it was for airplanes.

We need to fall faster.

He lowered the wings, still fully extended, so that they were fanned out behind him, and straightened his body like the shaft of an arrow. Molly's added mass created additional resistance, but almost right away, the tumbling ceased, transitioning into a wobbly dive.

The sea now began to rush up even faster, and the faster they fell, the straighter they flew. Molly shouted again, but whether it was a cry of elation or a frantic warning for him to pull up, he couldn't say. He maintained the near-vertical trajectory, trying to build up as much speed as possible, like an eagle diving for a fish just beneath the surface of a lake, and then, when the water seemed almost close enough to touch, he opened the wings and twisted the control handles to raise their leading edges.

The shift was so abrupt, Dodge felt his stomach drop. Molly's grip grew even tighter and for a fleeting moment, he feared that the shearing force of the turn might rip her lose, but somehow she held on. The dive flattened out and instead of falling, they were gliding a dozen feet above the blue-green infinity of the sea.

Dodge lifted the wings a little more and they began to climb but he could also feel the effects of drag, slowing them down. With a little time to practice, he probably would have been able to become as adept a flyer as any of Novotny's hawkmen, but time was something he didn't have. He angled toward shore, which seemed impossibly far away, and flattened out again.

"Dodge!" Molly's shout was perfectly audible now. "Above you."

Careful not to change the position of the wings, he twisted his head around to see what had caught Molly's attention, and groaned when he saw one of the Me-109s break formation to investigate the piece of falling debris that that somehow avoided splashing into the sea.

It would be on them in seconds, and with barely enough speed to stay aloft, there was nothing Dodge could do to evade the predator.

So much for soaring like an eagle, Dodge thought. We're more like sitting ducks.

He turned his gaze forward again, hoping that Molly had disposed of the djed according to plan so that the Germans wouldn't be able to retrieve it from their bullet ridden corpses. The distinctive chatter of distant machine gun fire reverberated across the water. Dodge gritted his teeth in expectation of the impact that would knock him out of the sky and end this last adventure. At least it would end with Molly's arms around him.

She let out another cry and for a moment he wondered if she had been hit. He craned his head around again and saw that Me-109 was now heading the opposite direction, pursued by a line of black streaks, starkly visible against the dawn sky. The shots hadn't come from the fighter plane; someone else was shooting at it.

He banked in the direction of the outgoing machine gun fire and saw the raked bow of a warship slicing through the sea ahead of them. A Vickers gun mounted amidships continued to hurl lead after the retreating fighter. Painted on the ship's side, big enough to be seen from a mile away, was the designation H35.

It was the *HMS Hunter*, the same ship that had brought Newcombe, along with Professor Dunn and Sadiki, to Egypt.

Dodge angled toward the vessel, trying to eke out a little more speed and distance. He didn't know if they would make it all the way, but he could see the Hunter's sailors moving about on the deck, making preparations to fish them out.

It wasn't quite the glorious end to the adventure he might have hoped for, but he would still be in Molly's arms, and that was good enough.

EPILOGUE— QUIET, NO TALKING

Dodge rushes out of the fire and charges up the steps, even as Boroff, pierced through with the rapier in Molly's hand, falls back onto the stairs, gasping out his last breath.

Molly turns, her eyes wide in surprise and joy. "Oh, Dodge! You're alive!"

Dodge closes the distance, and despite the flames rising up behind them and the smoke filling the great hall, wraps his arms around her. After a moment, he holds her at arm's length. "We won't be for long if we don't get moving."

He reaches out and catches hold of a dangling rope, then hugs her tight again. "Hold on!"

They swing out together, the flames lapping at their feet, and land on the far side of the hall next to Hurricane Hurley.

"Hurricane!" Molly shrugs out of Dodge's embrace and throws her arms around the big man.

"I'm like a bad penny, Miss Molly. I always turn up. Now, let's get out of here before we get roasted."

He turns and with a powerful roar, punches his fist into the heavy wooden door that blocks their escape. The door topples over with a crash like thunder, and then the three of them race across the drawbridge as flames vomit from the castle keep behind them. The bridge is quickly engulfed by the fast moving inferno, and as they reach the far side, it collapses and falls into the seemingly bottomless moat. Behind them, the entire castle collapses in a glorious fiery eruption.

Dodge and Molly stand together, holding hands and gazing down into the precipice, and as the music climbs to a triumphant crescendo....

Molly leaned over and whispered in his ear, the words almost perfectly synchronized with the dialogue of the actress on the screen. "I love you, Dodge Dalton."

He turned, looked into her eyes which glistened a little with reflected light. "I love you, Molly Rose Shannon, and I'm never letting go of you again."

A massive hand clapped down on Dodge's shoulder, another just like it landed on Molly's, and something like the low rumble of distant waterfall sounded in Dodge's ear. "Hush, you kids. Some folks are trying to enjoy this love story."

The admonition was in no way serious. The words "The End" had already appeared on the screen, and the capacity audience gathered at Radio City Music Hall—New York's preeminent cinema venue—had already broken into thunderous applause. Dodge and Molly joined in.

The last few weeks had been good for both of them. They were now closer to each other than ever, and their lives were finally back on track. Molly was back at University, intent on finishing her formal medical training. Dodge was working with Hurricane and a magazine publisher to develop a new series of high-adventure novels, and Liz Sansom had already staked her claim on adapting the stories for the big screen.

Not everyone had walked away from that long night with a good story and a happy ending worthy of a Hollywood motion picture. Fiona and Newcombe, along with Sadiki and a full military escort, had returned to Ain Della to recover the remains of Padraig Dunn and see to his burial. Dunn, who had lived much of his life investigating the tombs of Egypt, was laid to rest not far from them.

On Molly's advice, Dodge had not insisted on accompanying them.

"Fiona needs to grieve," she told him. "And she won't do that if she's constantly surrounded by people. Findlay will provide all the comfort she needs. Trust me on this."

"I do," he assured her. Molly knew exactly what Fiona was going through.

When the final curtain fell over the stage, Dodge and Molly joined Hurricane in the line filing out of the theater. The buzz of conversation was so loud, they had to wait until they were outside to talk about the experience.

"Liz did a great job," Molly said.

Dodge had to admit that it was true. Even though it was a little strange watching other people portraying himself and his close friends, the dialogue and performances had been spot on. Liz Sansom had perfectly captured their essence during their brief time together. Even more amazing was the turnaround time on the project. It seemed like only a few weeks had passed since they had bid farewell to the screenwriter upon returning to the United States.

Liz's script, which she had mostly written during the trip home, had been so well received that it had not only been fast-tracked into production, but bumped up from the low-budget serial division and made into a full-length feature which, an elated Liz had informed him during a telephone call relating the news, was the Hollywood equivalent of a miracle.

"Too bad she didn't take my advice," Hurricane said, unable to suppress a grin.

"Your advice?" Dodge asked.

"To make me the hero."

"You'll always be my hero," Molly told him, and then stood on her tiptoes to give him a peck on the cheek.

Hurricane blushed, and then stepped out to the edge of the sidewalk to hail a cab for them.

Molly stepped in close to Dodge, wrapping her arms around his waist. "Are you sure you won't get bored? Writing adventure stories instead of living them?"

He answered without hesitation. "All stories should have happy endings. I think we've both earned ours."

"Yeah, but—"

He pressed his lips against hers, silencing the question. After a few seconds, he drew back, smiling. "The End."

She nodded.

"Mr. Dalton?"

His smile faltered a little. It had been too much to hope that he would go unrecognized at the debut of a film in which he—or someone with his name—was the main protagonist. He turned, wondering if the man who had called out to him was a journalist wanting an interview or a fan wanting an autograph.

It was neither.

A man in black suit, wearing a fedora, proffered an envelope. "Read this, sir. Then I'll need you to come with me."

Dodge squared his shoulders. "Sorry, pal. I'm enjoying a night with my girl. You can reach me at the office the morning."

"Sir," the man repeated, shaking the envelope. "You really need to read it."

Dodge was about to repeat his request, employing slightly more assertive language, when he caught a glimpse of the embossed seal on the envelope.

Hurricane appeared at Dodge's elbow. "There a problem here?"

Dodge didn't answer. He took the envelope, glanced at the seal again to confirm that it was what he thought it was, and then took out the folded sheet of paper inside.

He refolded it, stuffed it back into the envelope, and then turned to Molly. "I'm sorry," he said. "I have to go."

ABOUT THE AUTHORS

SEAN ELLIS is the author of the Nick Kismet Adventures, Mira Raiden Adventures, Dodge Dalton adventures, and many other titles. He is a veteran of Operation Enduring Freedom, and has a Bachelor of Science degree in Natural Resources Policy from Oregon State University. He lives in Arizona, where he divides his time between writing, adventure sports, and trying to figure out how to save the world. You can find out more about Sean at his website: www.seanellisthrillers.webs.com.

KERRY FREY is the former Director of the Adventure Writer's Competition, sponsored by the Clive Cussler Collector's Society. In that role, he played a minor part in launching several author's careers that have led to the sales of over 200,000 books world-wide by the finalists of the competition. He lives in Mansfield, Texas with his wife Carol. He spends most of his time with family, friends, church members, or at his computer writing adventure novels. You can visit Kerry's web page at: aceroberts.com

www.ingramcontent.com/pod-product-compliance
Lightning Source LLC
Chambersburg PA
CBHW032119170626
46808CB00006B/2021